The girl was easily within reach. Claire leant forward and ran the fingers of her left hand across the girl's breasts several times. The little pink tips pushed out, erect. Claire played with them until they were hard, and then stroked the hollow of the armpit that was nearer to her.

'What an adorable little girl she is. She is so pretty like this. She loves it when we make her kneel and wait for a whipping, doesn't she? It gets her so excited. I'll bet she's wet already.'

Forthcoming titles in the Nexus Classics series:

THE IMAGE

Jean de Berg

and other classic French stories of submission

Juan Muntaner

This book is a work of fiction.
In real life, make sure you practise safe sex.

The Image
Copyright © Les Editions de Minuit
Translated by Peter Darvill-Evans copyright © 1992 Nexus
First published in Great Britain in 1992 by Nexus

Anne and the Mirrors
An Education in Charme
Taken from Les Ecarlates, copyright © 1985 Pré-aux-Clercs/
Belfond
Translated by Sue Dyson copyright © 1991 Nexus
First published in Great Britain in 1991 by Nexus

First combined publication date 1992 ISBN 0 352 33006 6

This edition 1999
Published by Nexus
Thames Wharf Studios
Rainville Road
London W6 9HT

Typeset by TW Typesetting, Plymouth, Devon

Printed and bound by
Caledonian International Books

ISBN 0 352 33350 2

Contents

THE
IMAGE

Preface

by
Pauline Reage

Who is Jean de Berg?

This is a question that gives me an opportunity to air my speculations. And first of all it seems to me that what is least certain is that this little book was written by a man, as it too strongly embodies a female viewpoint.

While it is usually men who initiate their mistresses to the pleasures of the chain and the whip, to humiliation and torture, it is also true that men are not aware of all of the implications of what they are doing.

Men assume, in their innocence, that they are satisfying their pride or their thirst for power, or even that they are merely exercising the rights due to them as a result of natural innate superiority. We intellectual women compound this misconception by giving men the justification for these opinions: we insist that women are free, are the equals of men, will not let themselves be oppressed any longer – as if any of these things had anything to do with the subject!

A man in love, if his perceptions are at all subtle, soon realises the error of his preconceptions. He is the master, without a doubt: but only if his lover allows him to be. The dialectical nature of the transactions within a relationship are demonstrated most clearly in the understanding between master and slave. Even when in chains, on her knees and pleading for mercy, it is the woman who is in charge.

And she knows it. Her power increases in proportion to her apparent abasement. The more she lays herself open the more cards she holds until, at the extremity of her apparent powerlessness, just one look from her is enough to

3

stop the proceedings and make the entire scene crumble into dust.

Once both parties have understood this unspoken agreement, the game can continue. Now, however, its meaning is inverted: the slave, trailing at her master's heels, is in fact an all-powerful goddess, while he has become no more than her priest, fearful of making the slightest mistake. His function is only to perform the rituals of which she is the sacred object. If he slips from grace, the entire ceremony collapses.

All of which explains the motifs of this book: the formal, hieratic structures of the action, the rituals, the churchlike settings, the fetishistic attention to details. The photographs, minutely described, can be seen as religious images, a new series of stations of the Cross.

This story, like all love stories, is about two people. But in the beginning the woman is divided into two distinct characters: one who submits, and the other who inflicts. In this she reveals the bizarre dual nature of womankind: a woman may give herself to others, but in the end she is aware only of herself.

Thus men are naive to expect us to adore them: they mean almost nothing to us. A woman, like a man, can worship only that same dichotomous body, in turn caressed and beaten, loved and abused, subjected to every humiliation, but all her own. The man remains inviolate, complete but irrelevant. He is merely the supplicant, aspiring vainly to become one with his goddess.

The woman, too, is a supplicant, to the same extent and to the same goddess. But she is also the divine object of worship, her continued sacrifices are made to herself. She experiences a double pleasure, unknowable to the man, as she contemplates the subtle game of mirrors in which she sees herself endlessly violated and reborn.

P. R.

1

An Evening at the X's

It was at a party given by Monsieur and Madame X, on the boulevard Montparnasse, that I saw Claire again for the first time that summer. What struck me most about seeing her again was that she seemed not to have changed at all. It was as if I had left her just the previous night, although in fact I was sure I hadn't seen her for at least two or three years.

She showed not the slightest surprise at meeting me. She held out her hand and said 'Hello', just as if we had parted the day before. I replied 'Hello, Claire,' in the same tone of voice, or something like it.

And then I met other people, and shook other hands, mostly those of people whom I see frequently here and there, all of them vaguely connected with the literary or artistic scene. I had things to discuss with several of them, and I spent some time talking about business plans in informal meetings that assembled and dispersed throughout the evening.

There must have been about thirty people there, in the three adjoining rooms that overlook the boulevard. It must have been June, or perhaps the end of May. One of the tall sets of windows was wide open.

When I noticed Claire again she was alone, standing on the balcony outside the open windows, with her back against the parapet. She was looking into the room, but not in my direction. I turned to see what she was staring at. It was a group of three people, standing and chatting just inside the window. Two of them were young men, under thirty years

7

old, whom I didn't know, and the third was a younger woman, scarcely more than a girl, in a white dress. I didn't know her either.

I glanced again towards the balcony and found that Claire was now gazing at me. She smiled at me with an expression that I found curiously enigmatic; but perhaps it was just the shadow falling across her face that gave me that idea.

She was leaning against the parapet, her arms extended on each side of her body, her hands gripping the top rail.

She was beautiful. Everybody said she was beautiful. And, seeing her again that evening, I could only agree.

I went up to the doorway, but I didn't step on to the balcony. Claire didn't move. I watched the people on the boulevard behind her, strolling past brightly lit windows in the warm evening air. I made some inconsequential remark about the scene. Claire replied, agreeing vaguely.

I looked at her face and saw that once again she was gazing fixedly in the same direction as she had been looking earlier. I didn't want to turn and stare behind me to find out if the object of her attention was the group of people she had been looking at before, but I assumed that was the case because her face showed exactly the same expression as it had earlier – an expression that displayed no emotion at all.

I took a few steps along the balcony, which extended across the front of the whole building, and reached the next pair of windows, which were closed. Automatically I glanced through the glass and between the tulle curtains, into the room.

The party's hostess happened to be standing just inside the window, and our eyes met. She said something to me through the glass but I didn't understand, because I could hear not a sound and I could guess nothing from the movement of her lips. Madame X unbolted the windows and half opened one of them in order to repeat her comment, but the curtains muffled her voice. Annoyed, I slipped through the narrow opening and into the room so that I could converse with her. It turned out that she had only been asking, as a joke, why I had been hiding on the balcony.

8

Finding myself with nothing to say by way of conversation, I asked her about the girl in the white dress, whom I pointed out with a glance in her direction. But my hostess seemed to know nothing definite about her, or perhaps was not prepared to tell me anything. She said only that the girl was a friend of Claire's, that she had arrived that evening with Claire, and that it was impossible to extract more than two words from her.

It seemed to me that the two young men who were talking to her were not faring any better. She was staring at the floor, avoiding looking at either of them, and hardly speaking at all.

However, she was very pleasing to look at. She was slim, and her face was very pretty. In fact there was something very seductive about her, in spite of her demure appearance. Although she was obviously very young, her whole body radiated a sensuality that made me think of her as a young woman rather than as a girl. And yet her little white dress, short and simple, made her look almost like a child.

Madame X had to leave me to attend to her duties as hostess. I continued to observe the young woman, who kept her eyes downcast, and I clearly recalled the look that Claire had fixed on her. Although I couldn't see Claire from where I was standing I knew that she was still on the balcony, leaning against the railing, her arms outspread, her hands gripping the metal bar. Her expression had seemed intense and yet empty, as if she had been watching the screening of a film which she had directed and which could not possibly contain anything unexpected.

Claire was beautiful, as I have said, undoubtedly more striking and glamorous than her young friend in the white dress. But unlike the latter she had never seemed to me to be sensual. That had surprised me when I had first come to know her, but I had decided that it was precisely her impeccable beauty, her unblemished perfection, that prevented me from considering her as a potential lover. I needed to think that something about her, no matter how minor, was vulnerable, in order to stimulate in me the desire to win her.

I approached the open window as I had done before, but this time with a definite purpose. I looked out to the balcony. Claire was no longer there.

I took a few steps further, went through the windows, and looked to left and right. There was nobody along the entire length of the balcony. Worried lest my manoeuvre had been noticed, I pretended that I needed to take the air and I leant my elbows on the railing, idly watching the passers-by as they strolled along the boulevard, past the brightly lit windows, in the warm night air.

Later I found myself sitting in a group centred on the room's largest sofa. Everyone else was arguing about the latest publishing scandal, but I was taking advantage of the opportunity to study at closer quarters than previously the young woman in the white dress.

The more I observed her features and the shape of her body, the more she seemed to me to possess a gentle and shy grace, with the movements of a timid ballerina whose slight awkwardness serves only to accentuate her charms. She was offering a tray laden with drinks to a group of men who were clearly more interested in inspecting her than in helping themselves to the glasses. Her dress had a full skirt and a cinched waist. The wide neckline revealed most of her shoulders, which were rounded, shining and lightly tanned.

'And what about you, Jean be Berg? You're not taking sides?'

It was Monsieur X, dragging me back to the spirited discussion. As I turned to face him I suddenly noticed Claire. She was watching me; her gaze remained resting calmly on me. She was leaning against the wall on the far side of the room, smoking a cigarette, alone, aloof, standing next to an empty chair. She gave me a brief smile which seemed to me to be the same enigmatic smile she had used earlier.

Later still, as I was getting ready to take my leave, I noticed Claire making her way towards me with a deliberate manner.

10

'I'm going,' she said. 'We could have a drink somewhere, to recover from all this, if you like.'

She spoke as if she were granting an indulgence that I had persistently been craving. I didn't reply immediately, as I was trying to think how I could establish whether her young friend would accompany us. But Claire herself added quickly: 'You can meet Anne. You'll see: she's very agreeable.'

She stressed the word 'agreeable' so that it sounded abnormal. I stared at her.

'Anne?' I said, raising my eyebrows.

'Yes. That little girl.' She pointed impolitely at the younger woman, who was sitting alone in a chair only a few paces from us. She was staring at her hands which were folded in her lap.

'Who is she, anyway?' I asked, in the most casual voice I could muster.

'Just a young model,' Claire said condescendingly. I should have mentioned before now that Claire is a professional photographer.

'And?'

'Well,' Claire said simply, 'she belongs to me.'

We were the only customers in the small corner of the bar we had chosen. Claire had given our order immediately, having hardly waited for my answer and without so much as asking Anne. We were all to have mineral water. The waiter served us quickly. Claire took an American cigarette from the packet I had put on the table, and lit it herself. She gazed at her friend and then leant towards her to rearrange a strand of her hair – fine blonde hair with highlights of gold.

'Pretty, isn't she?' Claire said in a provocative manner.

'Yes, very,' I replied, keeping my voice at the level of polite conversation.

'She's very pretty,' Claire repeated. 'And much more besides. You'll see.'

I looked at the girl. She didn't move or speak, but kept her eyes fixed on her glass of mineral water. Little bubbles intermittently detached themselves from the side of the glass and rose to the surface.

'You can touch her if you want to,' Claire said.

I looked at her. It occurred to me that she might be a little inebriated. But she seemed to be in her usual state of mind: cynical, which is how I had always known her.

'You'll see. It's very pleasant.'

I wondered again about her specific use of the future tense. Again I looked at the girl's smooth, round shoulder, dark alongside the white material of her dress. My right hand was resting on the back of the seat; I had to move it only slightly, and the tips of my fingers were stroking the golden skin.

The young woman trembled slightly and lifted her eyes towards me for a moment.

'Very pleasant,' I said, speaking to Anne.

'Her eyes are pretty, too,' Claire said quickly, and then whispered to the girl, 'Come on, look at monsieur so that he can see your eyes,' as she gently lifted the girl's chin with her closed fist.

Little Anne looked at me for a few seconds and then, blushing, lowered her eyes again. She had beautiful green eyes, very large and with long curved lashes.

Claire was now stroking Anne's face and talking to her softly, as if she were talking to herself. 'A beautiful mouth, too. Soft lips – soft and skilful. And pretty little teeth. Beautiful little white teeth. Let's have a little look at them.'

She opened Anne's mouth with her fingers.

'Stay like that!' she said, her voice suddenly sharp.

Anne obeyed like a good little girl, leaving her mouth half open to reveal two rows of even, brilliantly white teeth. Her face was turned towards Claire.

Her parted lips quivered. I thought she was about to start crying. I looked away and drank a few mouthfuls of mineral water.

'One day,' Claire said, 'I'll show you some photographs that I took of her.'

At this point I thought I heard the young woman pro-test, or at least give a low groan. She had said not a single word since the almost inaudible 'Monsieur' that had accompanied a charming little curtsey when we had been introduced. Now it seemed to me that she had just murmured 'Oh no!', or something of the sort, which caused me to speculate about the propriety of the photographs in question.

Claire, however, now seemed determined to leave immediately. As we were rising from the table, she said to me: 'Well, do you like her?' as if I were a prospective customer. She held the girl by the nape of the neck and pushed her towards me.

'She doesn't wear a bra, you know,' she said abruptly. 'I find it entertaining to make her go out without one.'

This time the girl blushed furiously. I was sure that Claire was about to announce another embarrassing revelation about another article of her friend's underclothing.

Contrary to my expectations she said nothing more on the subject and we went on to discuss only trivia, for the rest of that evening at least.

2

The Roses in the Bagatelle Gardens

Claire had arranged to meet me the following day: we were to spend the afternoon together, in the Bagatelle Gardens of the Bois de Boulogne. She had insisted that she had to show me the rose garden, which I had not seen before.

I now knew that I had no need to ask whether we would be accompanied by her young friend.

On the occasions on which we had met in the past Claire had never shown the slightest inclination to take me to public parks, nor to let me see any of her photographs. In fact until now she had never sought to meet me other than at the various gatherings at which we would bump into each other from time to time while spending a few hours in the same company.

For my part I had never made any moves to increase the familiarity of our relationship. As I have already mentioned, I found myself scarcely attracted to her perfect, regular, unassailable beauty. And I cannot recall having received from her the least encouragement to my friendly overtures at our first meeting. On the contrary, she had been distinctly cool.

As I waited for her on the terrace of the Hotel Royal, it occurred to me that I could not remember having seen her act differently with anyone else. She was always self-confident, reckless, even deliberately provocative. But she would immediately repel any hint of sentimentality with the same brusqueness with which she rejected more straightforward advances.

And on one occasion I had happened to be present when she cut dead one of her suitors. I thought then that I could detect a sort of loathing behind the icy determination with which she despatched him. The incident had shocked everyone present at the scene because the young man concerned had been a handsome fellow, of some sensitivity and intelligence, who was rumoured to be Claire's sometime lover.

I spotted little Anne coming towards me. She was wearing the same white dress she had worn the previous evening. In order to make her way between the other customers on the terrace she was obliged to insinuate herself between the tables and chairs, lifting her arms and turning her hips with the graceful undulations of a dancer. When she reached my table she executed her usual half-curtsey, a formal greeting such as is taught to little girls in religious institutions. Her voice, too, was that of a well-behaved schoolgirl.

'She is here, monsieur. She is waiting for you in the car.'

I was taken aback, not only because Claire's name had not figured in the announcement but also because of the exaggerated humility with which she had addressed me as 'monsieur'.

I rose and followed her. Claire's car was parked a little way off, in the rue de Rennes. Before we reached it I had time to ask the young woman two or three conversational questions, but she replied only 'Yes, monsieur' or 'No, monsieur' or 'I don't know, monsieur', as if she were indeed a little girl.

The car was a brand new black Citroën saloon. Anne opened the door and I said hello to Claire, who was sitting behind the wheel. Her only response was an almost imperceptible inclination of her head. I helped Anne into the car and sat beside her on the front seat, which was just wide enough for two.

Claire set off immediately, driving with calm precision. She navigated surely through the heavy traffic, and soon we reached less congested boulevards.

It was a beautiful day. The two women remained silent, staring straight ahead. Anne held her body upright, with her legs pressed together and her hands clasped on her knees.

I was sitting on the edge of the seat, against the door, in order not to take up too much room. I had placed my left arm, for support, along the back of the seat, behind the young woman. In doing so I had accidently touched Claire's shoulder, and she had recoiled instinctively. I had moved my hand away.

As I was, perforce, turned towards Anne, I could not help becoming aware of the perfume she was wearing. It was by no means overpowering, but it was noticeable because it seemed to be so little like her. It was sharp, compelling and very musky, the very essence of sensuality. It was certainly not a suitable perfume for such a young woman.

Without addressing anyone in particular I remarked that it was a beautiful day. No one replied. We drove on in silence. I had no particular interest in conversation, either.

We left the car at the entrance to the park and Claire led the way to the rose garden.

When we arrived Claire did not allow us to wander from flower to flower, but insisted that we admire the three or four varieties that she esteemed the most successful. She knew exactly where they were situated. They were all of the same type, with large but not very dense heads, well-separated and curled-back petals, and hearts still partially closed.

The most beautiful of all, according to our guide, was a bloom of a delicate shade of flesh pink which darkened towards the centre of the flower where the half-opened petals created a deep well of shadow. The very heart of the rose glowed an intense crimson.

After a few moments of rapt contemplation Claire quickly glanced from side to side. We were alone in this remote corner of the garden. The nearest people were about twenty metres away, and looking not in our direction but at a display of garish roses.

When I turned back to look at my two companions, I found that Claire had stopped admiring the pink rose, and was instead watching her friend. Anne was standing as if rooted to the spot at the edge of the flower bed, less than a metre from the rose, with her eyes downcast as usual. I was standing beside and a little behind Claire, and my gaze swept from the girl in the white dress to the flower, and back again to the girl.

Claire's voice broke the silence.

'Go towards it.'

The tone indicated that this was an order, calm but uncompromising, requiring obedience. It seemed to me that her voice had changed, however: it was deeper and more abrupt than when she had been directing us about the park or comparing the merits of various roses.

Anne did not ask what she was expected to do. After a momentary hesitation she glanced towards us, as if to reassure herself that our bodies were partially concealing her from the more frequented parts of the garden.

'Go on! Hurry up!' Claire told her.

She took a step forward, and her narrow shoes and high heels sank into the loose earth of the flower bed. I had not previously noticed that she had exceptionally delicate ankles. What could be seen of the rest of her legs appeared to be equally well formed.

'Now, caress it,' Claire said.

Anne stretched her right hand towards the half-open heart of the flower. With gentle fingers she touched the edges of the petals, hardly brushing the pink velvety flesh. She ran her fingertips round the central hollow of the flower, slowly, again and again. She carefully spread open the inner petals and then closed them again with the tips of her five fingers.

When she had spread and refolded the heart of the rose in this way two or three more times, she suddenly inserted her middle finger into it, so deeply that almost the whole digit was swallowed up by the dark hollow. Then, very slowly, she extracted her finger, only to plunge it once more into the shadow.

'She has pretty hands,' Claire said. 'Wouldn't you say?'

I concurred. I watched her hand. It was small, white and delicate, moving with grace and precision.

Claire was speaking in the same aggressive, cruel tone she had used in the café the previous evening. She threw a look of disdain towards the girl, who was still diligently caressing the interior of the rose.

'She enjoys that, you know. It excites her. We can prove it, if you like. The slightest thing makes her become wet. Isn't that so, little one?'

There was no answer.

'That's enough,' Claire said. 'Pick the flower and bring it here.'

Anne withdrew her hand, but then stood motionless, her arms at her side.

I turned to look back along the path we had taken from the central avenue: nobody was coming towards us, nobody was paying us the slightest attention.

'Well?' Claire said harshly. 'What are you waiting for?'

'I daren't,' the girl said. 'It's not allowed.'

She was so uncertain that her voice was hardly audible. Claire gave me an ironic smile, underlining for my benefit the foolishness of her pupil.

'Of course it's not allowed. Neither is walking in the flower beds, or touching the flowers. Didn't you see the notice at the gates of the park?'

Then, in a gentler, encouraging tone, Claire added: 'Everything that I like is not allowed, you know that.'

Anne started to reach for the flower's stiff stem, but drew back her hand.

'I don't know how to do it,' she said all in one breath. 'And anyway there are thorns.'

'So you'll get scratched,' Claire replied impatiently.

Once again the girl reached for the stem. She took it between her finger and thumb and snapped it off. Then she jumped backwards and, holding her prize in her fingers, she scurried towards Claire as if running for shelter from a sudden shower.

Separated from its plant the flower looked more beautiful than ever. Its shape was perfect, and the unblemished flesh of the petals had a texture that cried out to be caressed or tasted.

Claire expressed reluctant approval. 'Well done. You see, that wasn't so difficult, was it? But of course you will be punished, because you hesitated before doing it.'

The girl made no objection to this. Instead she lowered her eyes and blushed, the very picture of submission.

'What do you intend to do to her?' I asked.

'I haven't decided yet. But don't worry – she will be punished in your presence.'

Anne looked up, shaking her head, her eyes full of apprehension, as if she were about to plead for clemency. But her expression suddenly changed. 'Some people are coming!' she murmured.

'Well then, let's go,' Claire said, pointing to the far end of the path.

The girl, who had been hidden from the sight of the newcomers by our bodies, turned on her heels, and Claire and I fell into place on either side of her.

We continued with our stroll, three abreast, at a leisurely pace. Anne, in the middle, held the rose to her breast. As there was no one in front of us, no one could see the evidence of her crime.

As we passed the mutilated rose bush Claire turned to her young friend. 'Look, can you see your footprints?' she said.

The distinct shapes of two high-heeled shoes were imprinted in the soft earth.

We continued walking at a slightly faster pace.

We soon found ourselves in a clearing enclosed by undergrowth, private and completely deserted. As the area was devoid of flowers, we thought that we were unlikely to be disturbed.

Two iron garden seats, that looked reasonably comfortable, were set against a mass of foliage. Claire sat in one of them, and indicated that I should take the other.

'Sit down, Jean,' she said, and then, when I hesitated politely, she added: 'The little girl will have to stand. She has to hide what she's stolen.'

I sat in the chair beside Claire's. Anne stood before us, elegant and straight-backed, her white dress dappled with sunlight, the plucked rose held between her two hands and against her heart, her eyes lowered.

Claire and I looked at her for a long time.

The skirt of her dress, very full but cinched tightly at the waist, showed off the swell of her hips and the trimness of her figure. The wide neckline revealed the curves of her shoulders, and through the light material it could be seen that she was not wearing a bra. Or was that just my imagination?

At last Claire returned to her theme. 'You've got to hide that rose.'

The flower would have looked best against the girl's throat. She could have pinned it to her dress; it would have been easy to pretend that she had been wearing it when she came to the park. Unless, of course, the notice at the gates also forbade entrance to anyone wearing flowers. I looked for another solution, and saw a dense shrub on my left.

'All she has to do is to throw it under there,' I said, pointing to the bush. 'No one would think of looking for it there.'

'Obviously,' Claire said. She seemed irritated. 'But it would be a shame to lose such a beautiful flower. Wouldn't it, little one?'

'Yes. No. I don't know,' the girl replied.

There was another short silence, during which Claire studied her friend closely.

'It's quite simple,' Claire announced. 'You'll have to hide it somewhere about your person.'

When the girl did not seem to understand, because her clothes had no pockets and she was not carrying a handbag, Claire made her meaning clearer.

'Under your skirt,' she said, and then: 'You'll see. Come here!'

Anne went to her.

'Lift up your skirt,' Claire instructed, taking the rose from Anne's hands.

Anne leant forward to pick up the hem of her skirt and turned it up as far as her knees, presenting herself to Claire.

23

Claire burst out laughing. 'No, you little idiot! You've got to lift it all the way up.'

Anne blushed again, and glanced at me surreptitiously with her big green eyes. Then she looked carefully to her left and her right. She must have been reassured that we were in a relatively private place: even if someone happened to wander towards us, he wouldn't be able to make out what we were doing. She turned back to stand right in front of us and, holding the edge of her skirt in both hands, she exposed her legs to just above her round, smooth knees. Her sheer stockings were barely visible on her tanned skin.

'Hurry up!' Claire said.

As if stung by the lash of a whip, the girl revealed her thighs to us with one quick movement. Her full, pleated skirt was ideally suited to this operation: she could have lifted the hem up to her face without any difficulty. Her thighs were round and firm, and very agreeably proportioned. Above her stocking-tops, which were decorated with lace, the smooth, white skin contrasted with the narrow vertical strips of the black satin suspenders.

'Higher!' Claire ordered impatiently.

Anne gave me a look of complete despair, and this time she waited until my eyes met hers. Never had I seen such beautiful eyes, deep and serious, filled with fear and surrender.

Her mouth was open, just a little. Her breasts rose and fell with her quickened breathing. Her hands, which were now rolling the hem of her skirt up to the level of her waist, were far enough apart to afford an ample view.

As I had suspected the previous evening, she was wearing no knickers and no slip. Under her skirt she had only a little black suspender belt with a narrow ruffle of black lace, which formed a graceful arc over the short golden curls of her pubic hair. The mound of her sex was plump and prominent, small but softly inviting.

I looked up to catch the young woman's eyes, but they were now closed. She looked exactly like a tender sacrifice, calmly waiting to be offered up.

24

'Well,' Claire asked me, 'what do you think of that?'

I replied that I thought it most pleasant. I was particularly taken with the design of tiny roses against a background of delicate leaves that formed the tops of the stockings.

Claire was holding the rose in her left hand. She lifted it and stroked the golden pubic curls with the petals. Then she showed me the thin green stem, about twelve centimetres long.

'Look: the stem can be slipped between the suspender and the skin, just here, to one side of the crotch. The thorns will be strong enough to hold the flower in place.'

I disagreed. 'The thorns will only scratch the skin, and the flower will drop out as soon as she starts to walk.'

'Just wait and see,' Claire said.

She quickly examined the stem, and found only one large thorn, near the broken end. The rest were only brittle points, which she broke off with her fingernail.

'You see how nice I am to you?' she said to the girl. 'I'm taking off all the nasty prickles, so you won't get hurt.'

Then she suddenly turned to me. 'But I forgot. She's supposed to be punished, isn't she?'

Her voice became more authoritative and yet more tender as she addressed her friend. 'Move your legs apart and keep still. I'm going to hurt you. Come closer.'

Anne did as she was told. 'No. No, please,' she murmured softly even as she obeyed the instructions. 'Don't do that. Please don't.'

Claire held the rose by the end of the stem, with the flower downward, so that the single sharp thorn was uppermost, near the most sensitive flesh at the top of the inner thigh, next to the girl's sex. While the victim continued to say 'No, please. Don't do it, please,' Claire touched the steely point against the skin. Anne gave a little moan and bit her lower lip to stop herself crying out.

Claire waited a few seconds in this position, looking alternately at the girl's face and at the flesh destined for sacrifice. Then, quickly, she simultaneously pressed against the stem of the rose and jerked it downwards, making a small tear in the tender skin as the thorn penetrated the girl's flesh.

Anne gave a cry of pain from deep in her throat, and stumbled backwards. But she stayed in the same position, facing us, her sex exposed, her eyes wide and her mouth half open, even though her whole body was trembling.

Claire, still holding the rose, sat back in her chair and watched her victim with a look that seemed to me to contain either loathing or the deepest love.

For a long time the two women remained facing each other, neither making a move nor saying a word. Then Anne, still holding her dress up, took a step towards her mistress, returning to her previous position to offer herself again.

A tiny drop of blood, bright red, had formed on the naked flesh at the top of her thigh. Claire, whose expression was becoming kind and gentle, leant forward in her chair and placed a kiss on each of the girl's raised hands.

Then she used a finger to lift the black suspender belt, and with her other hand she inserted the stem of the rose beneath the material, sliding it towards the hip so that the flower protruded beneath the lacy ruffle. The thorn, now facing outwards, was used to hook the stem into the material of the suspender belt.

Claire sat back again to contemplate her work from a distance. She cocked her head and narrowed her eyes like an art connoisseur considering a painting.

'Now that's pretty,' she said to me, pouting. 'Wouldn't you agree?'

Beneath the central arc of lace the rose, held against the pale skin by its stem beneath the suspender belt, hung head downwards. Its upper petals covered a little of the black lace ruff, while the heart rested on the triangle of golden curls, hiding one of the upper corners. The edges of the lower petals reached almost to the top of one of the thighs. Lower still, between the point of the triangle, where the curling hair ended in a delicate feathery crest, and the black ribbon of a suspender, the drop of blood seemed about to run down the pearly skin.

I replied that the whole thing was a great success, although perhaps, I thought, rather overburdened with symbols from the romantic and surrealist movements.

Claire smiled. Her face was completely relaxed. She leant forward again, as if to adjust a detail of the composition, but instead started to caress the rose in the way she had ordered Anne to caress it earlier, spreading the petals and then plunging a finger into the heart.

She stopped suddenly. It seemed that she was only playing. She used the back of her index finger to stroke the short curls of golden hair.

'It's a shame I didn't bring my camera,' she said. 'This would have made a pretty colour photograph.'

She moved further forward and gently licked the red droplet which was threatening to run down the girl's thigh and mark the stocking.

Voices were approaching along the path beyond the bushes. Claire lifted her face to look at her friend with eyes full of nothing but affection. The two women smiled at each other for a long time.

It was a beautiful day. Anne's golden hair shone in the sunlight. In a peaceful voice that I had never heard from her before, Claire said: 'You may lower your dress.'

3

A Cup of Tea and its Consequences

We went to take tea at the pavilion in the park. Claire was lively, chattering, almost childlike. Even Anne spoke confidently and vivaciously. I could tell, from the evidence of this occasion, that she was in fact by no means brainless.

However our conversation touched only on trivial topics: gardening, art, literature. Claire made me tell her all about the scandal that she had heard me discussing the previous evening at the X's. Both young women seemed to find the story entertaining.

Little by little the carefree mood evaporated. The silences became longer and more frequent. Claire's face once again wore the closed expression it had at the beginning of our walk. The unmoving classic beauty of her features made me think of her again as a goddess exiled to Earth. I realised that she was again completely engrossed in her young companion, her pupil, her victim, her mirror. Anne, meanwhile, had resumed the modest demeanour of a mere object of lust.

We had finished our tea. Anne, with her hands in her lap, was arranging the pleats of her skirt into neat lines.

'Is the rose still in its proper place?' Claire demanded suddenly.

The girl bowed her head, indicating that it was.

'When you're sitting down like that,' Claire went on, 'the petals must surely fall into the valley between your thighs. They must be getting crushed. Is that what's happening?'

Anne nodded again.

'Then you must sit with your legs further apart, so that the flower can hang freely and not be damaged. Do you understand?'

The girl, unmoving from the waist upward and with her gaze fixed on her empty cup, carried out the instructions silently and rearranged the pleats of the skirt across her lap.

'Can you still feel the petals between your thighs?' Claire asked.

Anne nodded.

'And does it feel nice?' Claire went on.

Now the girl started to blush.

'Well? Are you incapable of speech?'

'Yes. It feels nice,' the girl said in a voice that was scarcely a whisper. Claire told the girl that if she could not speak more clearly in the future she would have her breasts exposed, there and then, in front of everybody.

'It would be very easy to do,' Claire said, turning to me. 'The gathered neckline of her dress is held in place only by a ribbon of elastic. And she's wearing nothing underneath.'

Putting her words into action Claire extended her hand to her friend's neck, grasped the edge of the material, and pulled it several centimetres lower. This was enough to reveal the entirety of one shoulder, the concavity of an armpit, and half of a breast.

She did not dare to continue until she exposed the tip. However the whiter, smoother and more intimate curves were plainly visible, stimulating thoughts of further indignities. Above this soft pale flesh an irregular pink line showed where the gathering of the elasticated neckline had left its mark on the skin.

'We're being watched,' I said. 'You'll have to stop there. What a pity.'

'Then let's get out of here,' Claire said irritably.

The three of us stood. Once she had restored her dress to its proper position, the girl went up to Claire and whispered something in her ear. Claire gave her a wicked smile, apparently pleased to have found a new torment so quickly.

'No,' Claire said in a loud voice. 'You can't go now. I can't be bothered to wait for you. You shouldn't have drunk all that tea.'

32

Anne followed us with her head meekly lowered. I had readily understood that she wanted to go to the toilet, and that she had been refused permission to do so.

However, I had as yet no idea what Claire was going to make of it. She began by nonchalantly leading us across the park, pointing out to us here and there a particular bed of flowers, a skilfully pruned example of topiary, the design of an avenue.

We came at last upon an area that was more wild and natural, without arcades or pergolas, where several tall trees had blanketed the unkempt grass with their fallen leaves.

This neglected part of the gardens would attract no visitors, particularly so late in the afternoon, with the setting sun lengthening and deepening the shadows. I assumed that our guide was seeking just such a secluded spot, as distant as possible from the well-used pathways.

And indeed Claire soon stopped and pointed out a russet carpet of leaves and broken twigs beneath a spreading beech. The tree's sweeping lower branches left ample space near the trunk but dipped their extremities almost to the level of the grass.

'This is the perfect place,' she said. 'Don't you think so?'

She had dragged both of us under the branches of the tree. On one side of the trunk was an open space, entirely enclosed by thick foliage.

'That depends what you want to use it for,' I replied.

'For the little girl, of course. She was looking for the toilets, wasn't she?'

'But – no,' Anne protested weakly, trying to lead the way back to the path. 'Honestly, I don't need anything.'

'In that case,' Claire said, 'why did you tell us lies, just a while ago? I thought you were going to give us a little performance.'

'No,' said the girl. 'No, honestly. I just made a mistake.'

Claire made the girl come and stand before her. She lifted Anne's chin with her fist and made the girl look into her eyes.

'Come on, you little idiot,' she said. 'Don't start making a fuss. You know that won't get you anywhere.' Her voice became rougher, still quiet but hard-edged with authority. 'You'll do it immediately,' she ordered, 'or I'll give you a slap!'

At once the girl bent her knees, carefully spread the skirt of her white dress all round her, and squatted before Claire. Claire reached down to stroke Anne's pretty face, which was red with embarrassment. With one hand she held her friend's face up towards hers; with the other she lingeringly caressed the girl's cheek, her eyelids and her mouth.

'Get on your knees,' Claire said in a gentler voice. 'That looks much more attractive.'

The girl knelt and, taking the white material in both hands, she gathered the folds of her skirt in front of her to keep them clear of her thighs. Just the toes of her shoes peeked out beneath the edge of the skirt behind her.

'Now then,' Claire said with a simper of distaste, 'shall we make the little girl have a pee?'

She used her fingers to unclench Anne's teeth, and started to play with the girl's lips. 'Make sure your legs are far enough apart!'

Anne moved her knees further apart. Her feet disappeared beneath her outspread skirt.

'That's better. Now lean forward a little.'

The girl leant towards Claire and lowered her head. Under the blonde curls that fell round her face, Claire's fingers were still fondling her half-open mouth.

'You look nice like that, you know,' Claire said. After a moment she suddenly lost her patience. 'Well? Get on and piss, you little bitch!'

Nothing happened. Claire immediately grasped the girl's hair in one hand, pulled up her head, and slapped her face with all the strength of the other hand. Once. Twice.

And then I heard the long-retained jet of liquid splashing violently on the dry, leaf-covered ground.

4

Wrong Moves

More than a week went by before I saw Claire or her friend again.

Then, on the eighth day, quite by chance, I happened to run into Anne in a bookshop in Montmartre. She was alone. She pretended not to recognise me which, under the circumstances, did not surprise me in the least.

I recalled the last image that had been imprinted on my mind that afternoon in the Bagatelle Gardens. It was the rose, which must have become unhooked from the suspender belt when Anne knelt beneath the beech tree: when she stumbled to her feet again, her face hidden in her hands, I saw the flesh-tinted flower lying abandoned among the dead leaves. It had fallen directly beneath the cascade: droplets of liquid still glittered in the hollows of its bruised petals. All around it the wet brown leaves gleamed dark and lustrous.

I had watched as one large teardrop slid slowly down a folded petal to fall on to a leaf that was still almost perfect, smooth and flat. The liquid spread across the leaf and created the appearance of a miniature mirror, which lasted for several seconds before disappearing.

Now the same young woman was speaking to the salesman. I was immediately struck by her decisive, self-assured manner as she dealt with the man. She wanted a rare book, a book that was, moreover, not generally available for sale. Nonetheless she asked for it with confidence, obviously sure that this was the place to find it.

The bookseller soon stopped pretending that he had never heard of the book, and withdrew a volume from a shelf concealed under the counter. Anne paid the amount that he asked.

I placed myself in her path by standing in the doorway. She could not avoid looking at me.

'Remember me?' I said.

She regarded me coldly. 'Obviously. But not in the way you mean.'

I realised at once that events were likely to follow a very different course on this occasion. I assured her that I meant nothing in particular, and followed her out of the shop.

'What do you want?' she said abruptly.

'Oh, nothing,' I replied. 'Just to have a chat with you . . .'

'I have no wish to be chatted with, and I'm in a hurry. I have to take this book back straight away.' She gestured with the little brown paper parcel that the salesman had made for her.

'To whom?' I said. 'To Claire?'

The look in her green eyes became even angrier, an icy gleam that was unlike any expression I had previously seen in her face.

'I will take it to whomsoever I choose,' she said. 'It's none of your business!'

I tried to extract myself from the confrontation with a knowing smile and a hasty farewell, but she had already turned and started to walk away.

The encounter left me highly dissatisfied.

I had by no means thought that I, in my own right, had any power over the young woman. However, it had seemed natural that I should enjoy certain privileges, even in Claire's absence: after all, I had already been granted considerable licence without having had to ask for it.

On further reflection I began to wonder whether I had been allowed so very much after all. I was obliged to come to a negative conclusion.

Finally I understood my mistake. I laughed inwardly at my stupidity, because Anne's recent behaviour suddenly appeared completely normal and obvious, and for her to have reacted differently seemed incomprehensible.

In short, the situation was not as I had imagined it.

I was annoyed. I felt I had been misled. I decided to forget about the two women and the whole ridiculous episode.

I waited three more days. On the fourth day I telephoned Claire.

I am convinced that she was waiting for my call, although her voice, at the other end of the line, betrayed nothing. In the most casual of conversational voices she asked me what I had been getting up to and how I was getting along since the last time we had met. I said I was getting along fine. Then I asked her how she was doing, and then I asked after her friend.

'But which friend do you mean?' Claire said.

'Anne, quite obviously. Are you trying to make a fool of me?'

'Anne! Ah, I see. I hadn't thought any more about that. If it's Anne you want to see, you should say so. I'll lend her to you, my dear, it's no trouble. You can play with her as much as you want, if that's what you fancy. What day would you like me to send her to you?'

There was a brutality in Claire's words that made me suspicious. Affecting indifference, I pretended that I thought she was joking and extricated myself from this awkward subject without specifying a day.

After I had hung up I reconsidered my idiotic behaviour. I wanted Anne very badly, that was certain. But I had to admit that I dreaded finding myself alone with the cold and distant girl I had met in the bookshop. She was so unapproachable that I doubted whether I could get anywhere with her. One might as well try to seduce Claire!

Or could it be that in choosing what was apparently the easiest option, that of rejecting Claire's offer of Anne, I was letting myself in for even more unusual delights? Perhaps it was this premonition that had, in spite of my desire, dictated my decision.

However that may be, in the end I had merely arranged a meeting with Claire, at her place on the rue Jacob, the pretext being to see the photographs that she had promised to show me.

Once again I recalled the girl in the white dress kneeling under the beech tree; the noise made by a stream of liquid splashing on dry leaves beneath her skirt; and the rose, with glittering beads still dripping from its bruised petals.

5

The Photographs

I recognised the photographs at first glance: they were on sale to the susceptible in the very bookshop in which I had met Anne.

On the other hand it had not appeared to me that Anne was known at the establishment; certainly the salesman who had served her had seemed not to have known her.

The prints which Claire showed me on the afternoon that I visited her were larger and of a far higher quality than the inferior copies through which I had absent-mindedly browsed one day while in Montmartre. On that occasion I had not been particularly struck by the images, and the poses had seemed rather ordinary.

This time, however, I saw them in a new light, and not only because I recognised little Anne as the model who had posed for them. The substandard prints I had seen previously had conveyed none of the extraordinary clarity of Claire's photographs, which seemed to be aggressively real, more true to life and almost more tangible than reality itself. This striking impression was perhaps the result of the lighting in the compositions, or of the pronounced contrast between the whites and the blacks which enhanced the definition of the lines and forms.

In spite of the differences, however, I was quite sure that these prints were made from the same photographs as the pictures I had once seen in the bookshop. Claire, in allowing the humiliated image of her friend to be bought and sold in this manner, must have experienced a pleasure similar to that of a slave trader. And, as I was beginning to

43

realise, she had from the start been seeking to experience new pleasures of the same order, with my help.

Seen from this perspective the photographs offered added value both to me and to Claire. I was also able to offer her my entirely sincere congratulations on the technical aspects of the photography.

We were at an arm's length from each other in two small but generously upholstered armchairs in front of a low table, beneath an adjustable standard lamp which could easily have served as a spotlight during the photographic sessions.

It was the first time that I had visited Claire's apartment on the rue Jacob. The moment I stepped through the door I had been pleasantly surprised by the cheerful decor and the modern furnishings of the room (which were typical of the whole apartment, as far as I could tell). The building itself was very old, and its staircase was dark and narrow.

To increase the sense of isolation from the outside world and to emphasise the contrast between the exterior of the building and the interior of the apartment, the heavy curtains were drawn across the windows even though it was daylight outside. Even if the windows had not overlooked one of the narrow and gloomy courtyards so typical of old apartment blocks, they would have admitted only a dreary illumination which would have been less bright and yet less intimate than the skilfully positioned artificial lighting in the room.

Claire handed the photographs to me one at a time, carefully examining each of them while I was looking at the preceding one. They were mounted on sheets of cardboard the size of sheets of business stationery. The glossy surface of each print was protected by a thin overlaid sheet that had to be folded back in order to see the image.

In the first photograph Anne is wearing a short black slip, and nothing else except stockings and a plain suspender belt like the one I had already admired in the Bagatelle Gardens. These stockings do not have lace trimming.

The girl is standing next to a column in the same pose

she adopted when Claire instructed her to hide the stolen rose under her skirt. This time, however, she is wearing no shoes, and instead of the dress she has only the slip. She is holding up the flimsy material with both hands, revealing her parted thighs and the bushy triangle of her sex. One of her legs is straight, while the other is slightly bent at the knee with the foot only just touching the floor.

The top of the slip is decorated with a lace insert, but this is difficult to see because of the folds of the material: the right shoulder-strap is not in place at all, the left has slipped off the shoulder, and the entire garment is twisted round the girl's body so that one breast is only half covered and the other is almost entirely exposed. The breasts are perfect: well shaped but set apart, and not too heavy, the brown haloes around the nipples being distinct but not too wide. The arms are well rounded and curvaceous.

The face, under the soft curls, is a great success: the eyes are consenting, the lips are parted, and the expression is sweet innocence mingled with absolute submission. The head is tilted to one side, towards the exposed breast and the slightly bent leg.

The lighting accentuates the dark shadows while softening and defining the lines. Visible illumination comes from a Gothic window of which only a part can be seen, in the background and at one side of the picture. The column in the foreground is, like the window frame, made of stone, and is about the same width as the hips of the girl standing next to it. Beside it, on the other side of the picture, the head of an iron bed can be seen. The floor consists of a chequered pattern of large black and white squares.

The second picture, taken at closer range, shows the whole bed. It is a single bed, made of iron and painted black. The blankets have been stripped off and the sheets are thoroughly rumpled. The ironwork of the two uprights, at the foot and the head, is ornate and old-fashioned: spirals of curving, twisting metal stems are held together by lighter-coloured rings that are almost certainly gilded.

The girl is wearing the same costume, but is without the

stockings, and the suspender belt. She is lying face down across the disordered sheets, turning slightly to one side so that one hip is lifted higher than the other. Her golden curls spill across the pillow in which her face is buried. Her right arm, bent upwards, frames her head; her left is extended towards the wall. At her side, where the slip is not supported by its shoulder-strap, it is possible to make out the shape of her breast beneath her armpit.

The black slip is, of course, well pulled up, this time at the back. The silky material has been gathered with careless artifice at the small of the back and around the hips, with the obvious purpose of displaying, like jewellery in a silk-lined case, a beautiful pair of buttocks. They are rounded and full, and parted in a very pleasing fashion. Their firm contours reveal pretty dimples which are accentuated by the girl's asymetric position. The thighs are parted to show only a pit of dark shadow. From the place where the knee is bent forward to form a point the left leg disappears beneath a fold of the sheet, and only the left foot can be seen, emerging from cover almost to touch the extended right leg.

The photograph is taken from a high elevation so as to display the buttocks to best advantage.

In the next photograph the girl is naked, with her hands chained behind her back, and kneeling on the black and white tiles. She is viewed in profile, from above. The picture consists only of the naked girl, on her knees on the bare floor, and the whip.

Her head is lowered. Her hair falls around her face, concealing it and exposing the nape of her neck, which is bent forward as far as is possible. The tip of one breast can be seen below the shoulder. The thighs are parallel and sloping backwards, while the torso is flexed forward, which makes the buttocks protrude most fetchingly, as if prepared for punishment. The wrists are bound together behind the back at waist height, with a slender chain of shining metal. An identical chain secures the ankles together.

The whip lies on the squared floor, near the little up-turned feet.

It is made of plaited leather, like the small whips used on dogs. From the narrow, flexible lash it becomes thicker and harder towards the part that is held, which is so rigid that it forms a short handle. The lash forms a motionless serpent on the floor, the thinnest tongue curling back on itself.

The girl is still naked and on her knees, and she is now chained to the foot of the bed. The picture is taken from behind her. The ankles are tightly bound together, but now crossed one over the other, which keeps the knees wide apart.

The arms are also held open, the hands lifted on either side of the blonde head and at the same level. The elbows are slightly bent, the right a little more so than the left. The wrists are secured, with the same metal chains, to the two extremities of the arch that forms the crown of the black ironwork.

The torso and the thighs are held vertically, but the whole body is slightly twisted to one side, perhaps because of the fatigue of holding the pose, so that one hip is thrust sideways. The head is hanging forward and to the right, almost resting on the shoulder.

The buttocks are marked with dark stripes, which are very distinct and well defined, criss-crossing the central divide. The relative prominence of each line indicates the force with which each blow of the whip was struck.

This image of little Anne, on her knees and chained in an uncomfortable position to the foot of her bed, is obviously made all the more poignant by the visible evidence of the cruel torments she has just experienced. The spirals of black ironwork create an elegant background.

The naked girl is bound to the stone column with thick ropes. She is standing, facing the camera, with her legs apart and her arms raised. Her eyes are covered by a black band. Her mouth is open in a scream, or she is perhaps grimacing in the extremity of her suffering.

The ankles are secured to the right and left sides of the base of the pillar, so that her legs are pulled wide apart and her knees are slightly bent. Her arms are pulled upwards and are visible only up to the elbows; her hands are presumably tied together behind the column.

The ropes bite deeply into her flesh. One crosses from the right armpit to the left side of the neck, securing the upper body. Others are tied round the arms and the ankles, while more grip each leg above and below the knee, pulling the legs back against the stone and as far apart as possible.

This tortured body which, to judge from the flexing of the muscles, is struggling desperately to escape from its bonds, bears two deep wounds from which blood flows freely.

One gash extends from the tip of the breast to the armpit, on the side unencumbered by ropes. The blood streams down the side of the body in rivulets of varying size which flow together and then separate again, spreading in an elaborate tracery that covers the hip and most of the stomach, reaching as far as the navel. A wide stream follows the line of the groin into the pubic hair.

The second wound is located lower, on the other side of the body. It pierces the belly just above the pubis, cuts across the groin and curves down to the inner part of the thigh. Blood pours from this incision in rivers, covering the whole skin as far as the ropes that are tied above the knee. There the torrent accumulates before pouring directly on to one of the white flagstones, where it forms a small pool.

This image has a horrible fascination, in spite of its exaggerated romanticism. However, it can only be a trick. The two wounds and the streams of blood must have been daubed in red paint on Anne's helpless body. The painting had been carried out carefully enough to deceive the casual onlooker, particularly as the victim's anguished contortions are thoroughly convincing.

Perhaps the illusion was undermined by the artistry that had gone into the fretwork tracery of blood, or by the obviously excessive fluidity of the streaming gore. In any case the harmonious structure of the girl's body, far from being obscured by its artificial covering, seems to appear in a new light.

The last photograph in the series is clearly the product of a similar contrivance. The girl's tortured body lies, apparently lifeless, on the black and white squares. She is still wearing nothing but the black band across her eyes.

She is lying on her right side, with the upper half of her body twisted so that her face is turned upwards, towards the camera. The right arm is alongside the body while the left is held above the head, covering the ear and bringing into prominence the shadowy armpit and the breast.

The right leg is slightly bent and the left even more so, the knee being pulled up in front of the body. The photograph has been taken from a position in which the inside of the right thigh, the buttocks, the pubic area and the surrounding soft flesh are all clearly visible and in strong light.

The blood from the wound in the belly flows across the exposed thigh and forms a pool on both sides of it. It looks as though the young woman has been stabbed to death.

A line of blood trickles from her half-open mouth, crosses her cheek and drips to the floor. Despite this the face seems peaceful, almost happy. The expression of the mouth could even be interpreted as a smile.

I noticed that this photograph has not been taken on the same day as the others, or at least some of the others. The paintwork which had streaked the breast could have been washed off between taking the previous shot and taking this one, but the whipmarks on the buttocks were also no longer visible, and such marks do not fade so quickly. Perhaps the photographs had not been taken in the order in which I had seen them? Or perhaps the charming stripes on the skin had been nothing but make-up, like the rest of the performance?

I was about to ask Claire about it when, turning towards her, I saw that she was holding another photograph in her hands. I had thought the series was complete, but she had taken another example from her portfolio.

She handed me the image. It immediately struck me as unlike the others. The quality of the printing was completely different, for one thing, but there were also other contrasts. Up to now each photograph had shown all of the subject, whereas in this one parts of the body had been cropped by the frame. The setting was no longer the austere Gothic chamber: this photograph had been taken in the very room in which we were sitting.

A woman, lying back in one of the small armchairs with her nightdress pulled up to her waist, is caressing the interior of her sex.

Because of the folds and rolls of the material of the garment, only the unclothed parts of the body can be seen clearly: the two arms, the hands, the lower stomach and the open thighs. The lower legs, the head and the shoulders are all outside the field of vision.

Both hands are between the widely spread thighs. The index and middle fingers of the left hand pull open one of the fleshy lips; the other is held open by the thumb and little finger of the right hand. The third finger of the right hand is pulled back; the index finger touches the tip of the clitoris, which is very obviously erect; lower, the middle finger is embedded up to the middle joint in the open orifice. Under the intense lighting the surface of the membranes glistens with secretions.

The dark, highly polished fingernail of the two hands finally gave me the clue. I remembered that Anne's fingernails were unvarnished. And everything about the pose, the position of the arms, every small detail, seemed to me less abandoned and less yielding than Anne. The pubic hair, too, was darker than Anne's.

I glanced towards Claire, intending to ask her if I knew the model who had posed for this photograph. Her expression surprised me: her face was flushed, she looked less severe than usual, and was obviously excited. Everything about her suddenly seemed more desirable than ever before. She was wearing a black jersey and tight pants; she was leaning back in her chair like the model in the photograph, and she let her hand wander to the junction of her thighs. Her fingernails shone with a vivid red varnish.

50

Suddenly I realised that she had just shown me a photograph of herself. She had presumably taken the shot with an automatically timed shutter release. The voluminous nightdress and the cropping of the face were calculated to allow her to add the photograph to the others without suggesting that the subject was a different person.

Without taking my eyes off Claire I placed the photograph on the table. I could not decide whether to move closer to her.

But Claire recovered her usual poise immediately. She rose abruptly from the armchair and turned on her heel to face me. It seemed that she was once again her usual self: severe, unbending, flawlessly beautiful.

She uttered not a word, but stared me straight in the eyes, disdainfully, as if waiting for me to say something.

'That last photograph,' I said, pointing to the table, 'is that still Anne?'

'Who do you think it is?' she replied drily, her voice suggesting that it would be unwise to pursue the matter.

6

A Propitiatory Sacrifice

Claire replaced the photographs in the folder. She seemed angry. I was at a loss to know how to coax her back into the mood of the silent moment we had shared while looking at the photographic image of her naked body. (I was still certain that she had been the model for the final picture.) The state that she had been thrown into, however briefly, by the idea of a man seeing her in such a revealing, excited, indecent position suggested to me interesting possibilities that had until then, in the light of her usual demeanour, been unthinkable.

But as soon as I heard her condescendingly polite voice asking me what I thought of her talents as a torturer I was once again overwhelmed with an awareness of how incapable I was of seducing her, or even of desiring her.

Little Anne was enough to satisfy her desire for humiliation. Anne was the prey that she offered to share with other hunters instead of offering herself to them.

I replied that her talent as a torturer seemed to me as great as her talents as a photographer, and that this should be taken as a considerable compliment.

'Thank you,' she said with an ironic smile and a slight inclination of her head.

But the exchange lacked lightness and spontaneity. Claire, having recovered from her inexplicable moment of weakness, was on the defensive and ready to bite. I had the impression that she was looking for a suitable opportunity to demonstrate her strength or her callousness.

'And my model,' she said, 'aren't you going to compliment me about her?'

I decided that in my reply I would be advised to refer only to Anne. I assured Claire that she certainly owned the most delectable of victims.

'You met her the other day, didn't you?' she asked me.

'Yes, in Montmartre. But she wasn't at all delectable then!'

'Really? Do go on.'

I thought for a few moments, trying to work out how much Claire knew of my encounter with Anne.

'She probably didn't feel like talking,' I said evasively.

'Did she fail to be respectful to you?'

'I didn't know that she was supposed to be,' I said and smiled, amused by the idea.

'She must be respectful to you, if that is what I require,' Claire said.

And I understood, at that point, the way things would be from then on. The only remaining problem was to guess exactly what Claire wanted: many and various things, no doubt, and all of them to be carried out in her presence.

For my part I was at first pulled along mainly because I was intrigued. But as soon as Anne came into the room, summoned by her friend in a voice full of threats that sounded like promises, I became aware of the reawakening of other sensations.

Claire and I had seated ourselves again in the two small and well-upholstered armchairs, which we had turned to face the middle of the carpet. The low table, which was no longer required, had been relegated to a corner of the room.

Anne was arraigned before us in the usual way: she was standing, her arms at her sides and her eyes downcast. She was wearing a pleated skirt and a blouse. She had no shoes on, and was in stockinged feet. She had been called in to explain the incident at the bookshop and to be punished forthwith if she deserved it.

Of course there was no question of needing to find out whether the young woman deserved punishment or not; this was simply a pretext for us to torture her as we chose while seeming to administer a justifiable punishment.

Claire was interrogating her with a vehemence that boded her no good, and it took only a few minutes for Claire to become convinced that there was evidence of grave insubordination on Anne's part.

It was decided, before the girl had had a chance to open her mouth to defend herself, that she should be chastised immediately.

'Undress!' Claire commanded.

Little Anne knew her part by heart, and did not need to be given specific instructions. Facing her mistress she dropped to her knees on the thick woollen carpet and removed her garments one by one. She was obviously performing a well-rehearsed ritual.

As it was a warm day she was wearing very little. She started with the skirt, which she unhooked at the waist, opened at the side, and pulled over her head.

As on previous occasions she was wearing no knickers. Her suspender belt was of pale blue satin, delicately trimmed with lace. She unbuttoned her short blouse, leaving it open at the front so that her breasts could be seen beneath the light material.

Then she unfastened her suspenders before removing her stockings, one at a time, lifting first one knee and then the other. She unhooked the catch at the back of her suspender belt and placed it on the carpet alongside the skirt and the two stockings.

She took off the blouse, the last vestige of her costume, and raised her arms to cover the upper part of her face.

She remained in this position, on her knees with her thighs parted and her body erect, completely exposed for our contemplation.

Her body was soft and full, slim but rounded and dimpled, and more desirable than ever. Her skin was smooth and an unvarying light gold in colour except where it paled on the stomach and breasts. The nipples appeared to have been lightly rouged. Although I was looking at the young woman from the front, I was reminded of the image which depicted her from behind: chained to the iron bed in a position similar to this, her buttocks striped with the marks of the whip. The expectant pose in which the victim was now holding herself was infused with extra significance by the memory of the photographs and of the tortures they contained.

Claire seemed to be prepared to go to any extreme, but at first she confined herself to making comments about the docile body in front of us: she remarked on the perfection of the shape and the gracefulness of the attitude, she spoke lengthy eulogies in praise of the firm breasts and the plump sex, she enthused over the soft flesh that was awaiting her whims and the delicate skin that she was already looking forward to damaging.

Claire proved to be not the slightest bit compassionate, despite these generous remarks. Her voice became increasingly violent and angry as she proceeded to list the forthcoming chastisements. Even the most fantastic of torments sounded ordinary to me as I recalled the tortures I had just seen convincingly staged in the photographs.

Claire interspersed her speech with carefully chosen obscenities, degrading insults, and humiliating intimate descriptions. At the height of her rage she suddenly fell silent.

After a long pause she spoke again, in a calmer voice.

'Get up, you little slut! Go and fetch the whip!'

The girl stood up, keeping one arm across her eyes. She turned and crossed the carpet to the door. She moved with a childlike grace that was incongruous with her nakedness. The two orbs of her buttocks, as yet unmarked and undulating with each step that she took, promised us the cruellest of pleasures.

Anne returned immediately, one of her forearms still covering the upper half of her face. In her other hand she held something made of leather. She dropped to her knees in front of Claire, and close enough to pass her the object, which was the braided whip I had seen in the photograph. Claire took it by the rigid handle, and then made her victim turn sideways in front of the chair, so that she was facing towards me. Without having to be given further instructions the girl moved her knees apart and lifted her arms. This time she raised her arms above her head so that we could see her delightfully fearful face and her pretty half-open mouth during the punishment.

Instead of striking the girl, however, Claire assumed a gentle manner. Her voice became softer. She was still itemising the particulars of various acts of cruelty, but she might have been murmuring words of love.

The girl was easily within reach. Claire leant forward and ran the fingers of her left hand across the girl's breasts, several times. The little pink tips pushed out, erect. Claire played with them until they were hard, and then stroked the hollow of the armpit that was nearer to her.

Claire's hand moved back to the nearer breast, and then down the girl's flank and across her hip to caress the insides of the thighs. Claire's voice was sugar sweet. She was speaking as if to a child.

'What an adorable little girl she is. She is so pretty like this. She loves it when we make her kneel and wait for a whipping, doesn't she? It gets her so excited. I'll bet she's wet already.'

Her inquisitive hand moved up to the girl's sex. The fingertips stroked two or three times along the slit, from the rear to the front. Meanwhile the other hand, still holding the whip, caressed the buttocks from behind.

Suddenly the index finger of the left hand, disappearing beneath the mound of golden curls, penetrated between the lips. With a single thrust the finger entered the humid cavern. Anne's eyes closed and her mouth opened a little wider.

Claire gave me a triumphant look. The ease of the penetration indicated the extent to which the girl was moist, aroused and ready for sex.

'You can see how thoroughly she has been broken in,' Claire said to me. 'When she knows she's going to be beaten, she gets ready to come. It's all down to training, just like with a dog. Once I'd played with her in this position often enough, she couldn't help enjoying it. Isn't that right, you little whore?'

At this point Claire, without removing her left hand from between the girl's thighs, delivered a sharp lash across the buttocks with the whip in her right hand. Her skill in manipulating the plaited leather indicated long hours of practice.

The girl jumped, and her arms instinctively dropped a little, but she raised them again immediately.

Claire struck her again.

'Look at Jean!' she ordered. 'You're being punished for his benefit.'

Anne lifted her face, holding her eyes wide open to avoid flinching at the strokes of the whip and concentrating on keeping her lips parted as Claire wished.

In order to deliver hard and well-placed blows to the soft flesh displayed before her, Claire was obliged to remove her left hand from the girl's sex. The lashes, now skilfully aimed, struck the buttocks in a regular rhythm, and each time the whip cracked against the skin the girl gave a little moan, an *Oh!* of pain that sounded like a gasp of ecstasy.

Claire began to strike more and more quickly, and the girl's cries came faster and faster: 'Oh! – Oh! – Oh! – Oh! –'

Then the girl's concentration slipped. She lowered one arm until it almost touched the floor; she sank back, halfway to sitting on her calves.

Claire stopped whipping. The girl was seized with fright and straightened her body, repositioning her knees and lifting her arms above her head again.

'Perhaps it would be better if she were tied up,' I said.

'Yes, if you like,' Claire replied.

At that point Anne started to cry, very quietly. The tears formed in the corners of her eyes and rolled down her flushed cheeks. Occasional shivers ran through her body. She tried to sniff as inconspicuously as possible.

Kneeling on the thick woollen carpet, her body straight, her thighs held apart, and with her hands in the air, she dared not move to wipe away the tears that trickled down her face.

We sat and watched her for a long time.

* * *

Anne was sent out again to fetch the metal chains. As she walked out her buttocks, crimsoned from their punishment, were more exciting than ever.

As soon as Anne stepped back into the studio Claire, who had left her armchair, pushed her to the floor on the pretext that she had not carried out her instructions with sufficient alacrity. Holding her victim's wrists together behind her back with one hand, Claire used the other with all her strength to slap Anne's face five or six times.

Anne began to weep twice as hard as she had before. Claire paid not the slightest attention, and dragged Anne across the carpet towards me, lashing her with the whip.

When Anne was in front of me Claire placed the chains around her wrists and ankles. Each chain was a length of strong chrome-plated steel links, ending at one end with a larger ring and at the other with a spring clasp. The clasp could be passed round a limb and through the ring to form a loop imprisoning the limb; the remaining length of chain could then be twisted once or twice round whatever support the limb was to be tied to, and the clasp could be hooked into a convenient link in the chain to keep the bond tight.

The system was quick and simple to use: within a few seconds the girl's hands were chained to the two arms of my chair, which were separated from the seat in a way that seemed designed for this purpose. The ankles were then bound together, one foot crossed over the other in the arrangement that prevented the thighs being pulled together and that I had already noticed in the photographs. Chained in this way the girl was obliged to lean forward, with her breasts between my knees and her blonde head close to my hands.

Very gently I caressed her tearstained face, and let my fingers wander down her neck to her breasts, her shoulders and her arms.

I asked Claire to continue the punishment, but now each stroke of the whip that landed on the bruised buttocks merely made the girl writhe in her bonds. It seemed that for the moment Claire was satisfied with seeing her friend reduced to helplessness. She was wielding the whip very carefully but slowly, almost gently.

I took Anne's slender neck in my hands again and made her lift her face towards mine. I leant forward and kissed her mouth. Her lips melted against mine. I drew back for a moment and tightened my grip on her throat.

'Kiss me better than that, you little whore,' I said, and pressed my mouth against hers. Her obedient lips and slim tongue started to move very pleasantly to the rhythm of my kisses as the leather whip cracked a little more loudly against her naked flesh.

When at last I pulled away and guided Anne's docile neck down towards my thighs, I noticed that Claire had pulled a cushion towards us and was half sitting on the edge of it with one leg folded beneath her. She had dropped the whip, and with her right hand she was carefully stroking the two rounded shapes of the girl's buttocks, which were marked with vivid pink stripes. I had a very agreeable view of them from my elevated position.

Claire's expert hand moved forward from the rear to the girl's sex, and once again penetrated the cleft. I heard Claire murmuring: 'She's soaking wet, the little sweetheart,' and, after a while, 'It's like a little lake in there.' Her thumb, easily finding the orifice, disappeared inside, withdrew and plunged in again. Anne began to moan.

Her cries became longer and harsher as the caresses continued and as Anne's hand moved back and forth between her thighs.

From my position I was unable to see exactly what her fingers were doing, but I judged from the girl's increasingly loud cries that Claire's activities were undeniably efficacious.

For a while I was content to play with Anne's warm lips and the tips of her breasts while I contemplated the rhythmic agitation of her lovely buttocks. Then it occurred to me that Claire could not have been no naive as to be unaware of the indecencies to which she had exposed her young friend by tying her to my chair in this position, and I released my sexual organ. I guided it towards the girl's overhanging face.

After an initial revulsion she surrendered to the inevitable, and compliantly rounded her lips. Her expertise indicated that this was certainly not her first such experience. I placed a hand on her neck so that with gentle pressure I could govern the up-and-down movements of her head.

When I could feel that the little bitch was soon going to reap the reward for her efforts, I called out to Claire.

'Start whipping her again, now!'

Claire leant back, with one knee on the cushion, and began to whip the bound girl furiously. She aimed the blows at the most sensitive areas, the insides of the thighs and between the anus and the vulva, which made the poor girl flinch convulsively and thoroughly delightfully.

To prevent her movements inconveniencing me I grasped her blonde head firmly with both hands, so that I could keep it motionless or move it up and down according to the requirements of my pleasure.

7

Taking Measurements

As I was leaving Claire's apartment she informed me that from now on I could have Anne whenever I wanted her, and that I could amuse myself with her however it pleased me to do so. If ever I decided that the young woman had been insufficiently obliging or had merely done something that was not quite to my satisfaction, she would be most severely punished.

These arrangements, which were made in the presence of the interested party in a bar near Saint-Sulpice, suited me perfectly.

I did not feel any need to exercise my new prerogatives immediately. During the days that followed we restricted ourselves to meeting for dinner, as a threesome. We chose restaurants, in the quieter parts of the city, which had intimate and relatively private corners where I could occasionally sample the more harmless of my privileges. With a critical eye Claire supervised her protégée's progress in the art of becoming a perfect slave.

Sometimes a waiter or an astonished customer would throw us an inquisitive glance in the middle of one of our wordless scenes, or would overhear one of our bizarre conversations. These hints of scandal, which served only to deepen Anne's embarrassment, added immeasurably to our enjoyment.

When these lessons aroused my desires to the point where I needed to find a release, we had recourse to the car, which would be parked in a deserted street and where I could have the girl kiss and caress me.

One afternoon during that week the girl's mistress allowed

me to have the girl to myself: I was to take her in the car to the centre of the city, where we were to go shopping for a few trifling items of lingerie which I was to choose for her.

Claire preferred narrow, lacy suspender belts and stockings with embroidered tops. She would allow only the skimpiest of bras, insisting on designs that supported the breasts from underneath rather than by covering them, and which thus left uncovered as much of the nipples as possible. As Anne was not permitted to wear knickers or a slip, we were restricted to choosing only three types of underwear.

At first I had thought that the fun would consist simply of watching Anne as she tried on the garments. However when I noticed, through the window of a shop on the Faubourg Saint-Honoré, the pretty face of the young woman behind the counter, I began to realise that the ramifications of the whole ritual could turn out to be even more interesting than I had anticipated.

Having been told by Claire that Anne had been soundly whipped that very morning (as a punishment, needless to say, for a very minor mistake), I began to picture the girl's humiliation in front of the astonished salesgirls whom I would invite to take measurements and offer opinions.

Claire had given me no further instructions, so from this point on everything was up to me. She must have decided not to accompany us so as not to complicate things: a couple is, in this situation, less open to suspicion and more in command. All we needed was to find an amenable salesgirl; young and pretty, as they usually are in the fashionable shops, and not too easily shocked. On the other hand it would not do if she were to become too actively involved in providing her services; she should be merely a witness, understanding and yet discreet.

The one I had spotted seemed suitable. The shop was quiet and luxurious, and filled with tempting creations. The young woman, who was waiting for customers behind a showcase and a display of pink underthings, was between twenty-five and thirty, dark-haired and shapely. She noticed that I was looking at her, and gave me an encouraging smile: it's always worth encouraging a male customer who's looking for feminine undies.

We went in.

The pretty sales assistant turned automatically to my companion to ask about our requirements, but it was I who answered, pointing to a white suspender belt that was displayed in the window. Anne, as usual, remained silent, with her eyes lowered.

The item was therefore presented to me for inspection, and was soon joined by several other garments, in similar style. I expressed my opinions about various features of each of them, explained exactly which I thought most suitable, and insisted that wide openings were required at the back and at the front. The sales assistant smiled understandingly, and went on to point out the quality of the different garments.

We continued to converse politely and naturally. She did not seem particularly surprised at my companion's quiet manner.

'This one,' I said, 'is in a way the most attractive. But it comes down a little too far: I'm afraid it might not reveal all of the triangle below the waist.'

The woman looked at me. She glanced at Anne, and then looked at me again.

I smiled at her. She returned my smile.

'That's less convenient, wouldn't you say?' I added.

'It wouldn't be at all uncomfortable to wear, monsieur.'

'Of course not, it wouldn't be uncomfortable to wear. But it might get in the way of the view. And of the hands, too.'

Her smile now became much less professional. She even blushed a little. I turned towards Anne.

'I think you ought to try it on.'

'Yes, if that's what you'd like,' Anne replied, but so quietly that I could not be certain that the salesgirl heard her or understood the significance of the manner in which she assented.

I said that we would take the opportunity to try on a matching bra at the same time. I described the type of garment that I required, and the salesgirl unhesitatingly brought out the most indecent that she had.

Having made my choice, I pretended that I needed to show the salesgirl the type of ruffled suspenders that Anne was wearing. I calmly lifted the hem of Anne's dress up to her thighs.

'They're like that, you see.'

The salesgirl stared at me, at last showing some surprise in spite of everything that had already happened. Then she turned her gaze on the smooth, soft flesh I was showing her.

'Yes, I see,' she replied simply.

I told Anne to hold up the dress herself, while I described the way in which the lace ruffles covered the suspenders and used my hands to demonstrate their elasticity.

'Lift your dress higher,' I said, 'and come closer to the light.'

Anne obeyed instantly. The salesgirl, who leant forward to look, had every opportunity to notice that her young customer was wearing no knickers. She cannot have failed to notice, either, the heavy perfume which Claire made Anne wear in her blonde pubic hair.

While Anne, in the changing room, was undressing in order to try on the suspender belt and bra, I stayed with the salesgirl and discussed the weather. She entered into this banal conversation quite easily, but her expression retained an element of bemusement and curiosity. I saw that we could take things a stage further.

I turned towards the changing room.

'Hello! Are you ready yet?'

There was no reply.

'Well then,' I went on in a kindly, fatherly tone, 'let's take a look.' I went to the closed curtain, drew it aside, closed it behind me, and found Anne.

She was all in white, and perfectly charming. She was wearing nothing but the new suspender belt and the new bra. Each was as delightfully immodest as the other. I pulled the young woman against me and kissed her.

A few moments passed. I decided to call in the salesgirl. I poked my head through the curtains.

'Would you mind coming here for a moment, please?'

She approached, looking me straight in the eye and smiling bravely.

The room was easily large enough for three. Anne was at one end of it, facing us, and the salesgirl stood next to me. Anne spread her arms so that we could see more easily. Instinctively she had opened her mouth a little and parted her knees. I took one of her wrists and lifted it higher. I made her turn her body slightly, to the right and then to the left.

'As you can see,' I said, 'both of them will do very well. But I think the waistband of the suspender belt needs to be taken in a little.'

The young woman stepped forward and inserted a finger between the waistband and the hollow of Anne's hip. I gained the impression that she was becoming more than a little affected by this unusual performance.

'Turn round!' I ordered Anne, releasing her wrist.

Anne hid her face in her hands and turned her back on us. The two globes of her buttocks framed by the arc of the suspender belt, were crisscrossed with a dozen long red lines that stood out clearly on the delicate skin. As the punishment had taken place several hours earlier, the overall colouring of the skin had disappeared. All that remained were the marks left by the lashes of the whip, still plainly visible on the pale flesh.

I looked at the pretty salesgirl, but she did not dare to meet my gaze. She was transfixed by this sudden revelation, as if touched by divine power. Her arm, which she had been extending towards Anne's waist in order to adjust the hooks of the fastening, had stopped moving, fixed halfway between her body and that of the revealed avatar which she was suddenly afraid even to touch.

On closer examination the red lines did not appear to be completely regular: instead each stroke of the lash had created a series of almost contiguous points which corresponded to the protrusions of the leather braiding and which showed precisely where the flesh had been bruised more deeply. Claire had obviously put a great deal of her strength and expertise into the blows. Some of the stripes were still clearly raised from the surrounding skin, and I was unable to resist running the tips of my fingers along them, either to ascertain their condition more fully, or to make Anne even more aware of the ignominy of her position, or perhaps to comfort her in her suffering.

'It's nothing much,' I said to the salesgirl. 'Don't give it another thought. She's had a bit of a whipping because she was a naughty little girl, that's all.'

We met our friend at five o'clock in a very dignified tea room where a few old ladies were conversing in hushed voices.

Claire had arrived before us and had chosen a table in the most suitable corner. The pleasure that I felt on seeing her again surprised me, but then I suddenly realised that the whole day would have been incomplete, would have had no meaning whatsoever, without her participation.

All I said, however, was that she looked beautiful, which was under the circumstances a notable thing for me to say.

She gazed at me in silence. She seemed to understand something, something distant, and briefly she gave me a knowing and completely unexpected smile. But then she demanded to be shown our purchases.

I gave her the paper carrier bag that Anne had placed on the table. Claire unwrapped the contents, giving her connoisseur's evaluation of the diverse advantages of the styles we had chosen.

As she spoke she used, as usual, the most coarse and humiliating expressions, which never failed to bring a blush to the fresh face of her young protégée. I was lost in admiration of the subtlety of the torments she was able to inflict in this way: only a woman could be capable of pinpointing the most vulnerable regions of her own sex with such knowing cruelty. The way that her words affected me led me to believe that I could expect even better things from her in the future.

Next she asked me to give an account of the shopping

expedition. I told her, briefly, of the most amusing incidents that had occurred in the changing room, and of the deep impression that had been made on the young salesgirl.

'And did the little girl behave herself?' Claire asked.

My own reply was an uncertain shrug. I suddenly felt like exacting further punishments.

And so Claire turned to her friend.

'You must have been happy, surely?' she said. 'Weren't you glad that everybody could see what a little whore you are? Well?' she added, more harshly. 'Answer me!'

'Yes. I was glad . . .'

'Glad about what?'

'I was glad . . . to show . . . that I had been whipped . . .'

Anne's voice was a barely audible murmur. I wondered whether she was repeating the words without paying attention to their meaning, or whether she really believed what she was saying.

'You enjoy being whipped?' her tormentor continued.

The obedient lips formed the word: 'Yes.'

'Stand up!' Claire ordered.

Claire was sitting opposite me. Anne was between us, on my left; when she stood up her thighs pressed against the edge of the table. Her back was towards the rear wall of the room.

'Put your hands on the table,' Claire went on, 'and lean forward. Open your legs. Bend your knees.'

The girl obeyed.

As no one could see what she was doing, Claire put her hand up Anne's dress, from behind. She immediately announced the results of her exploration.

'She's wet already, the little bitch. You only have to threaten to whip her! Would you like to verify the findings?'

I reached my hand under the dress, where it encountered two agile fingers moving in the moist, warm channel.

Once again I met Claire's gaze, warm and conspiratorial. She was already thinking of futher outrages.

* * *

The waiter, a very young man, arrived to take our order. I was obliged to remove my hand.

Claire, however, pushed her chair against the wall to make her position look more natural, and continued her disgraceful activities. Anne, close to panic, tried to stand up straight but did not dare to pull herself away from her friend's caresses. She therefore remained standing against the edge of the table, which she was desperately gripping with both hands, staring with a stupefied expression at the dumbfounded young waiter.

I took as long as I possibly could to give every last detail of our order. The waiter, moreover, seemed hardly able to understand me, because he could not drag his eyes from the pretty girl with the distracted face, staring eyes and open lips who was writhing in the grip of an invisible force on the other side of the table.

'That will be all for the moment,' I said at last, and the waiter fled in terror.

'Well, little one,' Claire asked gently, 'does that feel nice?'

'Let me go, please let me go,' Anne pleaded all in one breath.

But Claire continued. 'Which do you like better?' she asked. 'When I play with you or when I hurt you? Now then,' she added, turning to me, 'didn't you say that she had been naughty this afternoon?'

I confirmed that the girl deserved to be punished. Claire did not ask for any further explanation, and without doubt she realised that I had no real justification for my statement.

'Good,' she said, 'then let's make her cry.'

Anne's contortions became more and more anguished: her mistress was now torturing her under her dress.

After a few minutes, however, a waiter appeared with our tray, and Claire was obliged to withdraw her hand.

'Don't think you're going to get off that lightly,' Claire said. 'When would you like to visit me again, Jean?'

'Tomorrow evening,' I said, 'after dinner.'

'Good. We'll save this until tomorrow, then. You can sit down now.'

Anne dropped back into her chair.

The waiter, who was not the young man who had served us previously, paid no attention to us as he arranged the cups, plates and cutlery on the table.

Claire sniffed her fingers, and then put them under her friend's nose.

'Smell that,' she said. 'See how good you smell.'

The girl blushed again.

'Lick them!'

The girl opened her mouth and closed her lips around the tips of Claire's fingers, tasting her own odour as she suckled gently.

8

In the Bathroom

The following evening in the apartment on the rue Jacob, I found Claire wearing her favourite costume for indoors: clinging black slacks and a tight black sweater.

She greeted me in a very off-hand manner, or so it seemed to me; perhaps no more off-hand than usual, I suppose. In those days it was only when I was not with her that I could imagine her being less inaccessible. We each sat in an armchair. I did not ask after little Anne.

We exchanged a series of inconsequential remarks.

'It's getting hotter and hotter,' I said. 'You'd think it was the middle of August.'

Claire looked at me with the distant, supercilious expression I knew so well. Then a sudden thought must have occurred to her, because she gave me a smile that was friendly, albeit sardonic.

'I'm afraid my dear,' she said, 'that we are obliged to keep our clothes on. In our role, as I'm sure you understand, it's imperative.'

The word *our* sounded promising to me.

'Very true,' I replied. 'We have no choice. That's especially true in your case, no doubt?'

'Oh yes,' she readily agreed, 'it's particularly unavoidable for me.'

I sensed a hint of regret in her words. Her expression had become softer and less guarded. Once again I suspected that unfamiliar temptations were beckoning her.

And she was more attractive like that; she looked even more beautiful. I attempted to make an oblique approach.

'So you never find that you're at all too warm, all covered up like that?'

Claire stared straight at me, unwaveringly, as her expression hardened. Her eyes narrowed and the corners of her lips .drooped in an exaggerated smile of disdainful amusement.

'No,' she said, 'Never.'

She rose from her chair.

'The little girl must be ready by now,' she announced. 'Follow me!'

Her self-assurance had entirely returned.

The door that she opened, without first knocking, led into a room which I had not previously entered: the bathroom.

Both its vast dimensions and its luxurious modern fittings were unusual in old Parisian apartment blocks. It had certainly been installed recently, presumably by Claire. She must have sacrificed a whole room of the apartment to it.

In addition to the usual bathroom equipment, which was of powder-blue porcelain, the first thing that I noticed was a full-sized settee in one of the corners. The enormous blue bath, which was against the far wall, alongside and at a right angle to the settee, was panelled with the same white ceramic tiles as lined the walls.

Anne was standing in the bath, facing the door, using both hands to soap her body.

Instinctively she spread her fingers and moved her hands to try to cover her sex and her breasts, but one hard look from her mistress was enough to make her abandon this attempt at modesty. She removed her hands reluctantly, one at a time, and finally stood with her arms at her sides, the palms of her hands facing outward, and her head lowered.

Her skin, pale gold and pink, was glistening with soap bubbles which formed trails of white foam across her flesh. The delicate fullness of her body and limbs so cried out to be touched that I could already imagine the sensations of that warm, wet, slippery embrace, the supple curves sliding between my hands.

Claire pointed to the settee, and I stretched myself along it. She went to sit sideways on the opposite corner of the bath.

'Get on with it!' she said to her friend, who was still motionless and waiting.

Anne resumed the soaping of her body. Claire soon decided that the girl was not showing sufficient enthusiasm, and she started to direct the girl's activities, instructing her in the places that needed to be scrubbed, the positions which had to be assumed (supposedly to make the task easier), and the extent and speed of even the slightest movement.

The entire body was dealt with in meticulous detail. Facing first one way and then the other, standing straight and then bent over, with one leg lifted or with her thighs widely parted, with her hands behind her head to stroke her neck, or massaging her breasts, or lingering between her buttocks, Anne had to perform all the motions of washing herself in front of us. Claire, of course, delighted in instructing her to repeat the most intimate and embarrassing movements.

Two or three times, under the pretext of making her directions clearer, Claire offered the assistance of her own expert fingers. She undertook these operations gravely and with an unwavering precision that almost concealed her growing excitement. I could easily see, however, that she was directing and handling her protégée with increasing harshness.

The little girl was a model of docility, even when obliged to endure protracted and uncomfortable poses, extensive probings, and spectacular contortions.

When she finally allowed the girl to sink into the water for the last time, Claire pulled up her sleeves and leant over the bath to wash away the last traces of soap from the body's most secret recesses. She expended a great deal of time and care. Her friend's body, immersed in liquid, responded to the slightest touch. Claire could turn her over and back again, extend, bend, open and close her limbs. Anne's body was lifeless, ideally flexible.

Without leaving the settee I pulled myself closer to the bath. Anne's head was at my end of it. Her mistress had placed her hands around Anne's neck and was squeezing it, pretending that she wanted to force Anne's head under the water.

Claire was smiling, but in the green eyes of the girl I detected a growing flicker of fear that could not have been other than genuine.

Nonetheless she obeyed the order to close her eyes and to hide her hands behind her back, in order to demonstrate more clearly her role as a helpless victim.

Claire continued very gently to submerge Anne's face.

Anne abandoned herself to it.

It was at that precise moment that Claire's bare arms claimed my attention. They were well formed, as I had expected, but I had not imagined that I would find them so exquisite.

Claire soon realised that I was studying her and not her victim. She returned my look, staring insistently, trying to make me shift my gaze.

Instead I smiled at her. I told her that she had very attractive arms.

She released her grip and stood up. As might easily have been predicted, her discomposure served only to increase her ferocity towards Anne.

'Get up!' she ordered.

As soon as the girl was standing, Claire made her spread apart her legs and put her hands behind her back.

'Don't move!'

The girl's lovely body was streaming with water. Her hair hung in sinuous strands against her neck and across half of her face.

'Would you like to see the little fountain?' Claire asked me, as if it were a challenge.

'Why not?' I replied.

'Watch this!'

She seized a handful of the girl's dripping pubic hair, parted the labia and thrust her fingers inside. In her haste she must have hurt the young woman, who flinched. Claire told her to keep still, threatening her with more mistreatment if she disobeyed.

'Show monsieur the pretty fountain,' she said, in a menacing tone that could hardly have been more at variance with the childish expression.

The girl needed no further persuasion. She bent her knees slightly and pushed out her chest. She closed her eyes. She clenched her hands in position at the small of her back. The colourless liquid gushed between Claire's fingers and fell into the bathwater below with the sound of a rushing brook.

For a moment Claire played with the lips of the girl's sex, and then with the stream of liquid. She let it land on the palm of her hand and redirected it to trickle down one of the girl's thighs.

I must confess that I found the whole scene, so marvellously sweet and simple, surprisingly charming.

9

The Gothic Chamber

Claire spent some time rinsing her friend's soiled body under a shower of warm water and then, all care and kindness, helped her from the bath. She rubbed, patted and polished with the towel.

She brushed and combed the small triangle of pubic hairs, and then used an atomiser to spray perfume on it and on the breasts, the armpits, the neck, the undersides of the buttocks and the cleft between them.

She dried the girl's hair quickly, with an electric hair-dryer and very carefully applied a bright pink rouge to the mouth and the nipples.

She seemed to be overflowing with tenderness, concerned only to adorn, beautify and pamper the young woman. She had no qualms about kneeling before the girl on the pale blue foam-rubber mat, and in that position she took every opportunity to kiss her favourite parts of the girl's body.

She behaved like a mother, a lady's maid, a child playing with a doll, as she carried out her self-imposed tasks, and all the while she maintained for my benefit a running commentary, and asked my advice about which perfume and which shade of rouge to choose.

When all the preparations were finished she dressed the girl in stockings with embroidered tops, and the white suspender belt and bra that I had bought the previous day. She made her masterpiece do a turn before her while she carried out a final inspection, and then she pushed the girl towards the settee.

'Go and kiss your master, who loves you.'

The girl came and placed herself next to me, almost lying beside me, and kissed me at great length on my mouth with all the patience and gentleness that I had already experienced. I pressed my arm against the small of her back to hold her closer to my body.

My hand then crept up her spine and stopped at her neck, so that I could control the contact of our lips, and the pressure and duration of our kisses, without having to move my own head. The girl started to make unconscious movements with her hips, a slow undulation that I could feel as it spread to every part of her body, pressed close alongside mine.

I suddenly wanted to look at Claire. I pulled the blonde head away from mine and rested the girl's face on my shoulder.

Claire's eyes flickered from the girl's swaying rump to my hand clasping the girl's neck, and then met my gaze. Anne was now kissing my throat.

I could see that her mistress found our embrace disconcerting. Suddenly she had no part in the proceedings. I prolonged her ordeal for some time.

And as I continued to let Anne kiss me while I watched Claire's face, Claire reached the limit of her patience. She came to stand near the settee, less than two metres from us, not knowing whether to separate us or to join in.

When I finally disentangled myself from the girl, and pushed her away, Claire made her stand up so that she could sit next to me herself.

'Come on, you little bitch. What do you think you're up to? Jean's here to watch you being punished. You can kiss him later, if he wants to, after we've made you suffer.'

'Of course,' I said calmly. 'Why don't we make a start?'

The ritual proceeded: the victim first had to kneel on the tiled floor before her tormentors to be told the particulars of the tortures that she would suffer.

She would be bound against one of the columns in the torture chamber. She would be whipped across the front of her thighs and on the lower part of her belly. Then she would be burnt with little red-hot needles in the most sensitive parts of her body. Finally her breasts would be whipped.

Claire, in a voice which she had difficulty in keeping level, asked me if I had ever used this type of needle to torture a woman.

'You'll see,' she said. 'It's very entertaining. It leaves hardly a mark, and the pricking isn't the least bit dangerous because the points are sterilised by the flames. But above all it hurts terribly – doesn't it, little one? – and it can be applied over and over again in the same places, indefinitely, without lessening the effect.'

The Gothic chamber was exactly as I had seen it in the photographs: the iron bed, the paving stones of alternating white and black, the two stone pillars supporting the vaulted part of the high ceiling, the narrow recessed window now covered by velvet curtains.

The diffuse illumination came from wall lamps and three adjustable spotlights with their beams directed upwards. The whole room, which was both austere and intimate, had something of the atmosphere of a chapel, and was by no means the kind of room that one would expect to find in an apartment.

There were also two leather armchairs, set close together. Claire and I sat in them.

Claire was thirsty. Anne, of course, was sent to fetch the drinks, still wearing the embroidered stockings, without shoes, the white bra and the white suspender belt whose styling obligingly left exposed everything that one might wish to see.

The girl had to kneel before us to serve us our drinks, and remain in the same position, awaiting our pleasure, while we drank.

Her pose was the one I had already seen her adopt: thighs apart, body held erect, arms raised, lips open. Her huge green eyes shone with a deep, almost unnatural brilliance that recalled the ecstasies of Christian martyrs from previous centuries.

All three of us were well aware that the punishments scheduled for the evening were by no means imaginary. The thought that in a little while the most sensual spasms of pain would be wrenched from this innocent, acquiescent young woman made her body appear even more desirable. I made her come closer so that I could run my fingertips gently across the curves and hollows which we were looking forward to torturing, without pity, for as long as it entertained us to do so.

Her sex was still moist, presumably the result of our kisses in the bathroom, unless, as Claire maintained, the humiliation of her pose, the indecencies that she was forced to accept, and the anticipation of the torture were enough to excite her.

I wanted to arouse her further, by stimulating specific parts of her body, but then it occurred to me that given her unhappy plight it would be more enjoyable to watch her do it herself.

'Shall we make her play with herself first?' I asked Claire.

Claire agreed, of course. But first she wanted to blindfold the girl's eyes with the black band. Anne was ordered to stand up and fetch the blindfold, as well as the prescribed whip, from a corner of the room where they were displayed on a low sideboard. She presented them to her mistress and resumed her position.

Claire showed the items to me. The whip was not the one that I had seen used before: instead of a braid it consisted of only a simple lash, more supple and more cutting. Claire tried it immediately on the girl's thighs. Anne winced and turned her head aside. A thin red line appeared across her smooth flesh.

'The little bitch chose a good one,' Claire said. 'She bought it herself, this morning.'

The blindfold was a wide ribbon of black velvet, made into a loop with a piece of elasticated material. Claire placed it across the girl's eyes as a charming finishing touch to the costume.

Still on her knees, and with one of the spotlights trained

on her, Anne was ordered to play with herself. She started with the undersides of her breasts, and then her hands moved to the little rouge-tinted tips, left exposed by the bra. Then she had to caress the interior of her sex beneath the arc of white lace. She was made to use both hands, so that she could open herself without her fingers getting in the way of the view.

While this was going on we quietly finished our drinks.

Claire and I turned to face each other at the same moment, as if we had planned the movement. I was thinking of the last of the series of photographs, the one for which Anne had not been the model but which depicted a scene similar to the one before us.

I realised that Claire was thinking about the same thing, and that she knew I was thinking about it too. Her face was in shadow, but I could tell that her expression was once again troubled.

Anne could see nothing, because of the blindfold. I stood up without making any noise, and leant over Claire's armchair. She turned her startled face towards mine, and I kissed her, first brushing her lips with mine and then covering her mouth, which began to soften under my kiss.

'Leave me alone!' she cried out suddenly, jumping to her feet.

As if to exorcise these unwelcome emotions, which had not been part of her plans, she turned on the kneeling girl. She seized the whip and began lashing the girl's thighs, from the front, while insisting that her victim continued with her handiwork.

'Play with yourself, you little whore!' she said as she wielded the whip, but under the rain of blows the girl instead stopped.

Claire started to strike her again. 'Play with yourself!' The girl, frantic with fear, immediately resumed her activities. 'Better than that!' Claire said, landing a sharp cut across both thighs.

At the end of her patience, Claire finally threw herself to the floor and frenziedly started caressing the girl.

Anne was lying on her back, with her knees lifted and her arms stretched out across the floor on each side of her head. Claire had one knee on the ground and was bent over her prey.

Very soon long moans were issuing from the girl, and moments later she lost all control, crying out continuously from deep within her throat, her mouth wide open and her head thrown back.

'Look,' Claire murmured. 'See how beautiful she is when she's coming, the little slut.'

I watched the girl's rhythmic movements. She tossed her head from side to side, clenching her hands. Then she thrust out her legs and in one motion turned on her side with her knees drawn up, and remained still on the black and white floor.

Claire, standing over her, pushed her with the point of her shoe, as if she were a corpse.

Claire was still not satisfied, however. She found it necessary to tear from the girl's body the bra, the suspender belt and the stockings, so that she was naked but for the black blindfold over her eyes.

With lashes of the whip Claire made the girl resume her position on her knees in front of my chair. She ordered the girl to begin caressing herself again, and added one humiliating and very pleasurable refinement.

'Play with your little arsehole, at the same time!'

Anne obeyed, one of her hands disappearing behind her back. This region of her body must have been very sensitive, because she very soon became more excited than ever.

This time, however, instead of bringing the work to its conclusion, Claire grabbed the girl and dragged her to one of the columns, placing her with her back against the stone.

In no time the girl was bound in position, her arms and legs forming an X and her hands and feet pulled back behind the pillar.

I directed the spotlights towards the scene and then moved closer. The girl's wrists and ankles were attached to each other by means of the diametrically opposed metal rings that were set into the four wide leather bracelets she was wearing.

I had seen such items on sale in Parisian novelty shops; they are sometimes worn by young women to demonstrate their devotion to their husbands. The upper rings came together at just the right height (a little under two metres) to stretch the girl's body as much as possible without causing injury.

Claire had resumed her ferocious manipulations, penetrating her victim with such violence that it was impossible to tell whether the cries she tore from the girl were cries of pain or of pleasure.

There was no such uncertainty when Claire recommenced the flagellation, striking at the girl's widely parted thighs and lower belly. The increasing vigour, accuracy and regularity of the carefully aimed blows made the girl writhe in every direction in spite of the tightness of her bonds. Her body looked so beautiful in the midst of its contortions that my enjoyment could only mount as the sacrifice continued.

Claire did not rest from whipping until her arm was tired. She then took the opportunity to place a gag in the prisoner's mouth before embarking on the next stage of the punishment, to prevent the girl's cries rousing the entire neighbourhood.

Then she brought within easy reach a small alcohol lamp mounted on an ironwork stand for ease of use. Having lit the wick she arranged the instruments in the flame by resting them on supports constructed for the purpose.

I admired the long metal needles. At one end each one was very thin and sharp, while at the other there was a narrow wooden handle which allowed the hot needle to be held without burning the hand.

When the metal was red hot, Claire skilfully carried out the torture: first one breast, then the other; then she moved to the upper parts of the thighs, concentrating on the areas that the lash had not reached.

She worked slowly, lovingly meting out the punishment, starting with a light touch on the surface of the skin and then pressing gradually until the sharp point was embedded about a millimetre into the flesh.

The girl's desperate writhings hindered the work somewhat, but the groans of agony that we could hear, even through the gag, more than compensated for the irritating difficulties that Claire encountered.

The victim's tears were now flowing freely from beneath the black blindfold and down her cheeks. Her breath came in panting gasps. When Claire returned to the breasts, concentrating on the rounded flesh near the armpits and on the area around the nipples, it seemed that the girl might almost break her limbs as she pulled at the metal rings that held her spreadeagled against the column.

I took up the whip and pushed Claire aside so that I could administer the last of the scheduled punishments, the whipping of the breasts. For a moment I stood and contemplated the young woman, completely at my mercy, who had at last ceased to struggle or to hope any longer for a reprieve.

I revelled in whipping her breasts. I swung the lash back and forth with all my strength, and stopped only when both globes were entirely covered in glowing red stripes.

'Untie her,' I told Claire. 'Take off the bracelets. And the gag. And the blindfold. Put her on the bed.'

Claire looked at me. Then, wordlessly and very gently, she started to undo the fastenings. Before bringing her friend to me she clasped her to her chest and kissed her at length on the mouth and eyelids. Then she placed her on the iron altar.

Anne remained still. She was lying on her right side, turned towards the wall, with her knees slightly bent. Her shoulders and buttocks had been bruised by the stone column during her punishment. I lay on the bed behind her and wrapped myself around her, my body moulding itself to hers.

With no thought for her I ravaged her, penetrating the smallest orifice of her body.

10

Everything Resolves Itself

That night I had a dream. I was entering the Gothic chamber again, but now it was wider and higher, like a church remembered from my childhood.

A naked girl is tied to each of the two columns; one is facing me, the other is turned away. I move closer. I know that both of them are dead, but still warm. Their bodies are pierced with a multitude of triangular stab wounds in all the most pleasing areas.

A drop of blood marks the location of each wound. I touch the blood with my finger: it is just starting to coagulate.

I lick the tip of my finger. The blood tastes pleasantly sweet, like a fruit syrup.

At that moment I notice another woman, stationary beneath an archway. Behind her is a window of brilliant stained glass. She is clothed in voluminous robes, like a Renaissance Madonna, and is seated on a throne. She extends her arm in a regal gesture of greeting. She has Claire's face. She smiles at me gently, with a distant, enigmatic smile.

As I walk towards her she seems to move further and further away.

I woke up. I, too, smiled: the dream was full of allegorical overtones but was clearly meaningless. Nonetheless I now felt that I should expect a visit from Claire, although she had breathed not a word about it the previous evening.

When I heard the doorbell ring, a little later, I knew at once that it was her. I had not yet dressed, so I threw on a dressing gown and went to answer the door.

Claire looked pale and tired. This morning her beauty was that of a wild animal caught in a trap.

'Good morning,' I said to her. 'And how is your little friend?'

Anne was feeling fine. She was still asleep, worn out by the previous evening's activities. Claire had looked after her like a mother, and in a few days there would be no marks left. Except, perhaps, a few lines on the breasts which would take longer to disappear.

'That's a shame.'

'Oh no,' Claire said, 'it looks very pretty.'

She spoke timidly, in a low voice, and seemed unwilling to meet my eyes. We were still in the hallway, and I was not at all sure what she expected to happen next.

'And what about you,' I said. 'How are you?'

She stared at me with wide eyes which she seemed unable to drag from my face. At last she lowered her gaze.

'I have come,' she said softly.

'Good,' I said. 'Follow me.'

In the bedroom I sat in the armchair and looked at her. She was standing near the bed, wearing a pleated skirt and a white blouse.

I gave her the order.

'Get undressed!'

She hesitated for only a moment. She knelt in front of me, on the sheepskin rug, and started to remove her garments one by one, according to the ritual. Her underwear was similar to that of her young friend. She was wearing no knickers.

When she was completely naked she parted her knees and raised her hands above her head.

I let her wait in this position for several minutes.

'Look at me!'

She lifted her eyes to my face.

'Do you like being on your knees?'

She lowered her head in assent. 'I am yours,' she murmured. 'You can do whatever you like with me.'

'Very good,' I said. 'Go and lie on the bed.'

She lay on her back across the rumpled sheets.

'Legs apart! Hands behind your back! Open your mouth!'

She obeyed without a word.

I stood up, undressed, and placed myself across her body. I put one of my hands behind her neck to keep her still.

'You've never been beaten?'

She shook her head, her eyes melting with anguish.

'In that case I'll be the first.'

I slapped her face, forehand and backhand, and then again. I looked at her for a long time, and told her that she was beautiful.

My hand reached down to her body, below her belly. There was overwhelming evidence of her state of arousal.

As I caressed her sex, I kissed her.

Then I raised myself on to one elbow and slapped her again, much harder, five or six times.

'Say "I love you",' I told her.

'I love you,' she repeated, and added that she was my slave and I could beat her to death if it pleased me.

I caressed her breasts and then her sex, at length and with great diligence. Then I made her lick my fingers.

I moved my mouth close to hers and told her to kiss me. She applied herself to the task with exemplary skill and docility. I did not return her kisses, but simply received her offerings.

Her lower lip was soft and tender, moist and warm. I bit it. Hurt and surprised, Claire could not restrain the instinctive movement of her head. But she immediately realised her mistake and brought her face close to mine again.

I slapped her, as a punishment, and ordered her to apologise.

'I beg your pardon,' she said, and I took her lip between my teeth again, nibbling and kissing alternately until tears appeared in the corners of her eyes.

I placed my hand between her thighs again. She was even more open and ready than she had been earlier.

As soon as I penetrated her she started to moan, calling out my name and saying over and over again that she loved me.

STORIES FROM
LES ECARLATES

Anne and the Mirrors

I

Anne's hands were covered in mud. She could feel the
dampness of the earth and the grass seeping through her
dress. Dew-drenched stems brushed against her face; the
harsh stones and nettles were making her knees sore, yet
a strange feeling of blessedness was rising from her belly
to her heart. She was playing the serpent 'to order'. The
footsteps she could hear behind her confirmed that she
was undoubtedly being watched with the same pleasure
that was slowly taking possession of her. The Archangel
had had this strange idea when they were standing on the
covered porch after the storm, looking at the sheet of
water stretching out at their feet. The last raindrops pierced the water, and it rippled like the lines on a face.
Above in the clouds, the thunder gave a long roar: the
last rumblings made the ground tremble. The Archangel
clasped Anne tightly to him. She was naked underneath
her dress. A smile slipped from the Archangel's eyes to
his lips, and his hand caressed Anne's wavy hair: at this
touch, she felt a shiver pass through her. Turning her face
away, Anne kissed the hollow of his caressing palm; then
she saw at her feet a lewd, sinuous slow-worm; the Archangel noticed it too. Anne guessed that he was about to
order her to emulate this bare finger, as it wriggled
through the mud; and the fear of this made her heart miss
a beat.

The Archangel murmured: 'Anne, if you love me, I want
to see you crawl across the grass to the château.'

He signalled to her to leave his side, and she walked

forward into the water. A cold hand seized her ankles; she did not turn her head.

'Must I begin here?' she asked, half praying.

'Yes,' the Archangel replied, softly. 'Go . . .'

Anne knelt down in the muddy puddle, lay full length on her stomach, and – using only her elbows to help her – began to move slowly towards the meadow she would have to cross in its entirety if she was to reach the château.

Now she was halfway there, covered with mud and soaked through. With every movement she made, her dress rode up around her thighs. Guessing what the Archangel was expecting, Anne slid forwards so adroitly that her snow-white buttocks came into view as the dress rode up under her belly. In the secret hollow of her flesh she felt the grass's lips, the gravel's teeth, and these slight wounds quickened her pleasure. She felt suddenly uneasy when an inner voice whispered: *You are dragging night's pink and black spider through the mud.*

The voice came back to her, from a long way away, like a light at the end of a tunnel, crying out above the din of an onrushing train: 'Mirror of death, mirror of death', then disappeared.

A sting from a clump of nettles brought Anne back to consciousness and to her role as snake-woman, swimming about half-naked in the green, grassy water. Her belly was on fire. She longed to hazard a glance at the Archangel, to see if the thick fruit whose stalk she had so often held in her mouth would move silently towards her and penetrate her loins. For if so, the torture would be over – if not, she had another hundred metres and more to cover. The effort alone occupied her whole mind, yet she recalled a scene which had cast a heavy spell on her the previous evening.

She was lying naked on her bed, her knees raised and her legs apart. The Archangel was sitting opposite her, staring hypnotically at the slender pink thread of her cunt. All of a sudden he leapt up, as though wounded, and roared out: 'Anne, Anne, you have stabbed me through and through with sparks!' A thunderstruck Archangel is sleeping between my velvet breasts, thought Anne after they had coupled. And it was her turn to stop being the slave and become the queen.

She crawled on slowly; leaden armour weighed down on her naked loins. All at once, this obstacle course seemed absurd to her, and she stopped completely, studying the still far-off goal. The French windows on the terrace were reflecting the sun: Jorg came out of the drawing-room, went to one of the tables and picked up a rain-soaked parasol which he opened up and shook. He looked at the meadow, where he no doubt saw his master, who was standing behind Anne. But not me, she thought with relief. He can't see me.

Still unmoving, she worked out the formula. I shall get up, ask the Archangel to have mercy on me, which he will do, and already she could feel the warmth of bathing in the hall of mirrors, already she could see herself cleansed, naked and white, covering her breasts and her legs with perfume.

When the spell of a game had been broken, she generally got away with it: the Archangel never forced her. But next time he would choose a more cruel game. Like the evening when he'd tied her naked to a tree in the park and whipped her, and not released her until dawn. In the night, the dogs had come close to her, unknown hands had caressed her ... In spite of that still-terrifying memory, Anne made up her mind. And then the Archangel laid his hand on her shoulder.

'Anne, if you're tired, give up ...'

She felt so much respect in that voice that she blushed. Is that the extent of my love, that it wears itself out so soon, she thought; am I going to be such a coward? With her nerves stretched to breaking point, maddened, unable to hold in her tears any longer, she dragged herself towards the terrace. Two obstacles which she feared still separated her from the château: a clayey area bordering the meadow, which had been turned into a sea of mud by the storm, and then the gravel path itself.

The mud-bath was worse than she had expected. For a moment she thought she would not be able to pull herself free of it, but the Archangel's voice came to her, still sweet and imploring:

'Anne, turn over and crawl the rest of the way on your back.'

She obeyed and then saw the Archangel: he was pale, and his penis was erect. He smiled at her, then lowered his eyes to her belly, and – in a voice grown suddenly harsh (Anne called it the voice of the wind) – he ordered:

'Go now. Go quickly!'

Feeling the skin tearing on her elbows, and moaning with the pain, Anne crossed the terrace, wriggling her shoulders, her loins, digging her heels into the ground to try to gain a foothold. Her dress had ridden up high on her body. At last she felt the hardness of the paving stones, and her head came up against the front wall of the château: she closed her eyes. When she opened them again, she saw the Archangel standing over her. A jet of liquid came raining down, each hot spurt defiling Anne's face and belly. The Archangel's eyes sought hers; there was so much sweetness and gratitude in his gaze that Anne felt she was bathed in joy.

She lay there, not moving, quite unaware of the fact that night was falling and the Archangel had long since gone back to his bedroom.

II

The windows of the great hall were open, and the last rays of the sun made the chandeliers gleam blood-red. The scent of the lindens on the terraces mingled with the weird, acrid fumes from a smouldering grass-fire. Anne stood before the tapestry which gave the château its name and its mystery, and tried to unravel the enigma of a scene which she had so often looked at. The moon-bathed Unicorn was white and softly padded. It stood erect in the bloody forest, between three long golden flowers. The Lady sat watching the thin sleeping dog with sidelong glance and cupped hand; in the distance, the eyes of the winged lion gleamed between the trees. Anne's eyes wandered towards the handmaidens, who were holding out caskets full of pearls and rubies. But there was a dark attraction for her in the enchanted beast with its dagger-like horn, standing erect amid the shadows.

Regretfully, Anne left the red and gold tapestry, still under the same spell, and returned reluctantly to a life in which she played both the victim and the queen.

As she passed a mirror, she caught sight of her lithe grace and stretched herself, pleased that she could treat herself to such a pretty sight. Her black velvet gown accentuated the whiteness of her shoulders, her half-exposed breasts, and her face with its waves of russet hair. She smiled to see herself looking so beautiful amid the décor of another age. Precious stones sparkled at her wrists: yet even they could not compete with her gold-flecked eyes.

Next time he comes, shall I be able to keep him here? But how can I know if he'll come today or tomorrow or at all? He often used to say, 'The Archangel will not come if he is summoned.' And so Anne waited from one second to the next in the star-shaped château which the Archangel had discovered, far from roads and villages.

Sometimes she wondered about her paradoxical lifestyle, in which she was overwhelmed yet unsatisfied, free and yet a prisoner, happy to receive the tokens of love and yet driven to desperation by her long, lonely days. And as for this fleeting, impenetrable being to whom she had bound her own life, who was he? Did she know?

One August evening he came into her garden. The setting sun cast a halo of bloody rays around his head; his eyes shone; when he spoke in low tones, there was a strange resonance in his voice. Anne was picking roses, and she offered him a flower without wanting to – already she was in the thrall of this man she would hitherto call the Archangel, or the Black Prince. At the end of the meal, the stranger asked for her hand in marriage. When she said yes, Anne wondered who had answered for her.

* * *

Had her childhood, perhaps, destined her for this bizarre marriage? The marriage ceremony took place at midnight in a chapel at the edge of the grounds. Standing white and erect in between the candles, Anne stole brief glances at the unknown, her husband. A smile highlighted the ironic twist of his lips, and the young woman thought: in marrying me, he's playing a bad joke on me! The discomfort of this thought did not leave her until the dawn, when she was awakened by the sound of birdsong filtering into the bedroom. She saw that she was lying naked, in the sleeping Archangel's arms.

Anne regretted the fact that her deceased parents couldn't come to her marriage: it would have surpassed all their hopes and dreams. Her father had passed on to her his taste for exceptional beings. He was a very learned man, who had devoted his life to the study of the secret sciences, and had chosen for his wife a creature who wandered between the earth and the heavens, talking incessantly of imaginary visitors and insisting – on alternate days – that her daughter was a horse, a flower or a star. Could her unsteady mind have been the victim of her husband's experiments? That's what people said. Anne often saw them spend the whole night locked away in a conservatory where her father kept his chemical apparatus and his powders.

Multicoloured gleams of light lit up the windows, and from time to time Anne heard her mother cry out; but she never knew what rigours were inflicted upon her by the old man with the emerald-green eyes.

And so she grew up amid the shadows which haunted her mother and the Hindu or Cossack magicians who came to visit the château. Although she had never been to school, by the age of twenty Anne knew more secrets than a lot of doctors. She was as enthusiastic about study as she would have been about pleasures and pastimes, if anyone had bothered to teach her any – and that's no doubt why the Archangel had chosen her on that summer night when an invisible guide had brought him to her.

Who could say what had become of her after eight years

108

of submission to her husband? Who would have recognised in that dazzlingly beautiful woman who cared only for her jewels and her beauty, that pure being that her father had once dedicated to study? In those days, he had often asked her:

'Anne, what do you expect from life, and what do you expect of yourself?'

The young girl had learned so well from the old man that she could speak only the truth, and her reply expressed her deepest desire:

'I don't expect riches or happiness from life, but I do expect myself to be strong enough to resist the lures of the world, so that one day I can attain wisdom.'

'So – do you think you have enough light in you to push back the darkness?'

'I am conscious of my nothingness, of my dark shadows,' Anne replied humbly. 'I am spurred on not by pride, but by the desire to know where the truth lies and how to reach it.'

This upbringing had enriched Anne's heart and mind, but the company of her mother was an inexhaustible source of both anguish and rapture.

This woman, whose beauty she had inherited, could make tables turn, talked to ghosts, covered herself in lace and perfumes, lived in a world of mirrors, sang old ballads like an angel and thought of Anne as a little cat – her familiar. The old man put up with his wife's extravagances. Anne, who admired her father, could never understand his indulgent attitude towards this delectable madwoman who would open the door of the drawing room and announce, confidentially, the last message she had received from Julius Caesar or Napoleon.

Shortly before his death, her father spoke out in a way which left a deep impression on his daughter. He warned her to be on her guard against a certain type of highly civilised beings, sent to earth by the forces of evil in order to keep men in their darkness. These beings should be feared by those who, like Anne, were taking the narrow path; for it was these people that they attacked. The old man finished with this command:

'Anne, never sleep! If you do you will be defenceless and all that I have awakened within you will be destroyed.'

A few days later, in the middle of the night, she heard her father calling her. When she entered his bedroom, she found him lying beside his wife. This waxen lady was singing quietly, with closed eyes; tears glistening in between her eyelashes. Anne approached the old man, who raised his arm to stop her.

'Don't say anything,' he said. 'My time has come. You are the guardian of our love. For us, the real task is beginning.'

The old man looked at her, smiled, and closed his eyes. At the very same moment, the waxen lady's song was cut short. All this happened before Easter. The following August, the Archangel appeared . . .

Leaning against the frame of the window which overlooked the terrace, Anne recalled those far-off days and always came back to the same question: was the Archangel one of these ill-omened beings against whom the old man had warned her to be on her guard, and did she still have a chance to escape from him?

In her dreams, a tall young woman walked along the corridors. Beautiful, terrified, doggedly seeking a treasure she never found, she opened doors which led into empty rooms, and trembled with anxiety. At the far end of the corridor stood the Archangel, smiling. The young woman tried not to look in his direction, and yet she kept on moving towards him. The treasure and the open doors were only a pretext, she knew that. Nearby stood an old man with emerald eyes. But a wall of sheer crystal separated him from his daughter, and he could not talk to her.

'If only there was another corridor,' moaned Anne, 'another way out other than the door where the Archangel is standing, waiting for me! And if his hand touches me . . .'

She remembered the last game – that stormy evening when the Archangel had made her crawl in the mud. When she went back to her room, her maid had taken care of her. After bathing, she massaged her bruised and battered flesh, covering her shoulders and her legs with perfume. Then she had put on a tulle negligée lined with satin, and silver slippers, and went downstairs to join her husband. During dinner, the Archangel made no mention of the affair, and neither did Anne. She was complimented on her choice of jewellery, and her husband's smile bore witness to his deep gratitude – and she could not hope for more than that.

She hadn't accepted this way of life, love and suffering without a fight. But the Archangel had seen deep into her whereas she only thought she knew herself, and in fact knew nothing at all. He knew how much slavery fascinated her. Before experiencing the promised sufferings, she lived in a state of terror. Yet, right from the moment when the first tears flowed, the pain never seemed so acute to her. She knew that the Archangel was watching her, knew that he loved her because of the sufferings that she accepted from him; and besides, in the end she got used to it. Nowadays, in the very midst of her cries and tears, Anne experienced undreamed-of joys.

After dinner, the Archangel asked her to choose some records and join him in the living-room, by the fire. Sitting side by side, taking turns to smoke the same cigarette, sharing the soothing rhythms, they were two lovers just like any others. The Archangel confided in her, talked about publication projects, told her how much he would like to travel in the East with Anne, and asked her advice. Surrounded by this tenderness which so rarely manifested itself, Anne forgot the nettles, the sea of mud, the way in which the Archangel had sought relief – never before had he entrusted the responsibility for his pleasure to any hands but hers. So why today? . . . Reading her thoughts, the Archangel explained softly: 'You were the serpent, Anne – every bit of you, from your head to your toes. You were the serpent, and I should have crushed your soiled belly, your reddened thighs. After all, you crush a serpent, don't you?'

Anne's murmured 'yes' was so faint that it was scarcely audible. The Archangel unbuttoned her gown and caressed her breasts. Anne let herself go completely. She was too

111

close to the fire, and her legs were getting burned, but she lay back in the encircling arms and surrendered her mouth to his, meeting the familiar scent of her lover. His flesh was imbued with a zestful mixture of lavender and English tobacco. She was tortured by the thought that she might lose him. Her hand stroked his curly hair – never before had she so desired to belong to him. Perhaps he would stay beside her until daybreak? Sometimes they had stayed like this, intertwined, when he had taken her by the fireside, or – more often – she would kneel with her face buried in her arms, supported by a low chair. Then he would ask her to thrust out her buttocks as far as she could: Anne flexed her small waist to show off her broad hips to best advantage. She put such an effort into disclosing herself that the dark, lined details of her flesh became visible. Sometimes, Anne felt the Archangel's hands caressing her; but often, when she wasn't expecting it, the whip would lash her. But by the fireside that evening, rocked in the Archangel's suddenly tender embrace, Anne thought that the first days of their love had returned. In those days they knew the spontaneous pleasures that come from the flesh, not the mind. Anne hoped to regain that lost simplicity: but alas, a sign from him left her in no doubt as to what was expected of her. The low chair, covered in grey satin, was moved nearer to the fire. Anne knelt down, her backside towards the flames, and hid her face in her arms; her fingers stroked the satin, and she leaned her cheek against it. Then, very gently, her gown was lifted up, and the tulle fell over her face like a ring of soft petals, turned inside out. Now she was locked in purple darkness, a prisoner of the veils she had chosen for their seductive power. She felt a wistful joy as she breathed in the perfume which impregnated her gown. This prison smelt of make-up and of the night.

Yet it was when she was covered like this that she offered herself best of all. With her waist arched backwards to the point of pain, she felt as though her naked loins belonged to some other woman, that the layers of material absolved her from the sins which might be committed by a part of her that she had a right to ignore. The Archangel knew this, and had noted it. He never took off his clothes, and lent himself without giving himself: for him, Anne's anonymous loins were enough to satisfy his desire. In these bitter, sad joys, the pleasure of one participant remained foreign to that of the other.

Then Anne heard her lover's voice. It was as soft as a caress:

'Anne: you who offer yourself to me completely, and whose tears I am about to call forth – I love you.'

And, at the touch of the gentle, exploring hand, Anne gave a moan of love and distress.

Her first cry was a brief one, but her loins were set on fire by the thongs, making them start and opening her flesh to the lashes that followed. Inside her upturned robe, she stifled her cries, bit her hands, scratched the satin with her nails, and tears flowed into her mouth. The Archangel, putting his weight behind his shoulders, whipped her burning rump with the other arm, using broad strokes. At last his stiffness entered her – so roughly that he hurt her. Anne cried out again; with her belly and loins pierced by daggers, she was at the same time snow and flames, and the proof of long-awaited pleasure sent her soaring beyond the limits of her own self.

As they lay, intertwined, by the hearth, sleep and dreams took them by surprise.

Anne could hear slow music as, along the avenues in the park, statues came down from their plinths and danced; one of them – a crinkly-bearded Moses clasping the tablets of the Law to his heart – was waltzing. The curving folds of his robes executed learned arabesques. He was saying these strange words over and over again: 'Next year's fashion collections will feature the prophetic draped look.' As he waltzed, he winked at Anne and – parting the folds of his robe – displayed the clustered fruit of his genitals. Even in repose, his penis seemed threateningly large and thick.

When Anne awoke, the Archangel was no longer beside her: on the table, she found a message informing her that her husband had been called to Paris, and could not say

113

when he would be back. It was a fortnight since then, with no news of him, and for that fortnight Anne had waited.

She shivered, realising that this evening too, the Archangel was not going to come. As she crossed the corridor, tiled with black marble, she thought fearfully of what awaited her: in that immense bed, the deep water where she would swim in her sleep, unceasingly groping for some firm, unyielding patch of water weed which she would never find . . .

III

At the top of the stairs Anne placed her hand on the rail and turned round. In the sleeping hall the suits of armour, the mirrors, the golden torches held aloft by turbanned negro boys, all were bathed in the shimmering water-effect. The French windows were still open, and a scent of earth and torrential rain was wafted up from the far side of the park. The faraway wind in the leaves imitated the sound of the sea.

Alone and turned to ice, Anne imagined herself abandoned forever. To escape from the loneliness of her room, she pushed open the first door at random: immediately, in the pearly light from the chandeliers, the carpet's pool of redness spattered across two marble columns. She found herself in the hall of mirrors – a strange room which seemed composed of blood, crystal and darkness. The Archangel spoke of it with a certain smile, calling it his 'fiery chapel'.

In her black dress, high-waisted like an Empire gown, Anne tried the effect of a ruby necklace against her shoulders. In this room, the Archangel kept the most beautiful jewels that he had given her. He liked to see her sparkling like a constellation, naked save for gold tiaras, her breasts bound with belts of precious stones, and to see her – thus bejewelled – multiplied by the mirrors' reflections. At first she refused to take part in these ambiguous games; to convince her, he had to tie her to a column and whip her. She recalled her rebellion on the day when the Archangel had

– in this very room – marked her for the first time. At that time, two years had elapsed since their marriage.

In the house which Anne had kept after her father's death, the Archangel worked hard, and with such skill that it caused her no distress, to erase all traces of the old man. At first, he professed the greatest respect for the secret studies which he himself had embarked upon, and it was because of his knowledge that he was able to win over Anne. It happened slowly, and by the lightest of touches.

'It's not wisdom that you're searching for,' he told her. 'Out of curiosity you want to unravel a secret.'

'If my father revealed so many things to me,' replied Anne, 'it was because he wanted to open the last door for me – the one that brings us, living, into the realm of eternity.'

'So you refuse life?' said the Archangel in astonishment. 'Then why did you marry me? How can you reconcile the duties which marriage imposes with these meditations, with all this reading which occupies your every waking moment?'

A few days later, he took up the theme again.

'What benefits are you getting in return for so much effort?' he asked. 'Has your dead father manifested himself anywhere but in your dreams? Has he given you a sign to prove to you that "the other side" – this kingdom you so want to reach – really offers all the wonderful things that are claimed for it?'

Anne admitted that she had received no sign.

'And yet,' the Archangel continued, 'if you were deprived of these Utopian researches your life would lose its attraction?'

'I believe so.'

'In that case, Anne, my beloved, your love for me is an unworthy one! I expected better of you. I thought you were unique enough to combine overwhelming beauty with a depth of passion which shows the quality of a soul. But if all I can do is arouse a lukewarm feeling in you, if I can't tear you away from your books, we shall have to split up! I won't share you. Not even with stars or spirits!'

When his voice changed tone like this, Anne shivered. She looked at her husband with admiration: he truly was the Black Prince she had seen glittering in the park on stormy days when she was a child. Now that she was a woman, the discovery of pleasure had increased the prestige of this god who took her to heaven every night.

'These ecstasies, these caresses: aren't they what happiness is all about?' said a voice in her ear – a voice which she thought was her own, but which merely repeated the words of the Archangel.

Pretty soon, she didn't even ask the question any more. One morning, she took her father's books up to the attic, forgot everything she had learned as she shut the door, ran to her husband and shared with him the ecstasy which she would henceforth prefer to any exaltation of the spirit.

That was the moment the Archangel chose to leave Aiguilleres and set up home with Anne in Paris. It was always open house at their fine residence near to the Bois de Boulogne. Fashionable people came to visit, and Anne's beauty caused a sensation. The newspapers praised her elegance, her distinction; the *Chronicle* noted her presence at gala evenings in the same breath as the names of famous film stars. Anne's discovery of society took her from surprise to delight. The Archangel sensed this new joy and – more still – the praise with which everyone surrounded his companion. That winter, they were Paris's ideal couple. Their names were not linked to any scandals, and – what's more – who could have embodied all the qualities which each of them offered to the other? The Archangel had one of the prettiest women of the moment, and Anne had one of the most fascinating, coveted men. The Archangel's publishing house prospered: and happiness – such a fragile word – assumed the dazzling form of their success and their pleasures.

Where did the break come, wondered Anne. Who tired first of this easy happiness? I did, she thought for a long time. But this evening she knew that the break had been initiated by the Archangel. And the moment when he showed her the evidence had no doubt been well chosen:

116

restlessness led to dizziness, their wasted time was crumbling away; one day, they would wake up and find that they had lost themselves. The Archangel did not have to be very persuasive to get Anne to come back with him when he discovered the château where she was waiting for him today. At first, Anne accompanied the Archangel to Paris. There, she met old friends and unchanged interiors: the theatre on dress-rehearsal nights, the bars on the Left Bank, the art galleries, the literary salons where everyone took credit for other people's words. Anne received the same praise everywhere, but she no longer felt pleasure in the company of these people who hid destitute minds under a veneer of wit. She preferred to withdraw with her husband to the studio which he had furnished, and spend the night there when they didn't want to make the journey back home. Eventually these trips became rarer. The Archangel began to invite some of his friends to the château; for Anne, these private receptions marked the beginning of slavery.

Three couples were invited to supper each Monday. The women were chosen for their beauty, and their faces were masked with feathers and flowers to emphasise their bird-like grace. Under their long dresses, they displayed their nakedness. The men were in dinner-jackets with black velvet masks, and were free to lift up the bird-women's dresses and present their nakedness to the rest of the party. But each person took his pleasure in seclusion, and only with the woman who accompanied him: so in these games, Anne experienced only the Archangel's caresses.

And yet, she recalled her shame when, one evening after dinner, a guest came up to her. Standing by the fireplace, she was pouring out the liqueurs when she felt two hands on her legs. Turning round, she saw the man on his knees, and – sitting on the couch – the Archangel, who signalled to her. She yielded, as he ordered. Her dress, which was made of layered petticoats of Flemish silk and black net, was lifted up by the guest, who then pinned the fabric up. So Anne had to finish the evening semi-naked. She saw another scene in her mind's eye: one of the female guests, whose dress had been pinned up by the Archangel, revealed, to everyone's surprise, two heavy, scarlet buttocks on which the whip had left its mark. The woman's companion then said that he had marked her in this way just before they arrived. All night, Anne was attracted by this burning mass whose brightness was revived, whenever it began to fade, with loud slaps . . .

Anne stood unmoving, dreaming, in the pearly light from the chandeliers. The mirrors looked across at each other from one wall to the other, at an angle specially chosen to create an infinite number of images of this bare-shouldered woman with heavy, red-gold hair, who was watching her ten attentive sisters and trying to populate this desert of mirrors single-handed.

She recalled one evening, when she was playing with her reflections in the same way as now, when the telephone bell called her to her bedroom. Instantly the voice of the Archangel was within her: it was a week since she had had any news of him.

'Where are you?' asked the Archangel.

'In my bedroom. Where are you?'

'Are you standing or sitting?' demanded the Archangel. 'Understand me – I want to *see* you.'

'I am sitting on my bed,' replied Anne. 'I'm looking at the window. I'm holding the receiver in my right hand and the phone in my other hand, on my knees.'

'Which dress are you wearing?'

'My midnight blue negligée.'

'Nothing else?'

'Nothing.'

'Right,' continued the Archangel's voice. 'Listen to me and do what I'm going to tell you to. Lie down, naked, on the fur rug. Put the receiver against your left ear, caress your right breast with your left hand and, with the other hand, trace the curves of your body and describe for me all that your hand meets. Do you understand?'

'Yes,' came Anne's docile murmur. 'Just a moment.'

The thin layers of fabric fell softly to the ground. Rounded and white, she rushed forward on her long legs and lay down, pressing her left ear against the receiver.

118

'OK,' she said. 'My left hand is stroking my right breast, and my right hand is holding my knee – but where are you?'

'I'm sitting in my office,' replied the Archangel. 'And I'm ready to follow you. Your words shall guide my caresses, and your voice is my pleasure.'

Anne, who had spent a week tasting the exhausting pleasures of expectation, was deeply moved by this voice: with its help, the desires of the Archangel slipped into her ear; the vibrations of this voice and this desire won over her heart. Breathlessly she gave herself with a newfound joy, murmuring softly:

'I'm alone, I'm cold, I love you. My right hand is leaving my knee, it's climbing up my thigh – which is just as broad and white as you could wish for, and soft too. It's sliding towards the inside of my thigh, where the skin is finer. My fingers are brushing against a little bush . . .'

'No,' ordered the Archangel. 'Take a different route. Move your hands towards your buttocks and roll over on your front so they are fully exposed.'

Anne could have pretended to obey him, talked as though she was giving in to his demands without actually doing anything. But she felt confused and unsettled, and submitting to his orders, she stretched herself out on her stomach.

'Are you ready?' asked the Archangel.

'Yes,' replied Anne. 'My right hand is on the back of my right thigh. Now it is moving upwards, making contact with a rounded hillock and following its sinuous lines . . .'

'Cut the crap,' said the Archangel tetchily. 'Slip your hand into the cleft and tell me what you are pushing apart.'

Anne begged him not to make her say it: she was ashamed of this word, and he knew it. But the Archangel was insistent and she began once more to speak.

'My hand is sliding into a tight little furrow, burrowing down, and parting my . . .'

'Your what?' snarled the Archangel.

'. . . Parting the cheeks of my arse,' Anne whispered almost inaudibly. Then she heard the Archangel's breathing suddenly becoming more excited and felt exhilarated. She began again. 'My white, hard, cold bum-cheeks which you love so much, and which I am giving to you, and which I am shaking as though you were whipping them, and which I am slapping – listen: can you hear me?'

Anne moved the receiver close to her backside, and with the other hand rained down a shower of loud slaps on her buttocks. Then she spoke into the receiver again.

'Did you hear that? Answer me . . .'

'I love you, Anne, I love you,' sighed the Archangel. 'But hit yourself harder and for longer – I want to hear a hundred and fifty slaps.'

'A hundred . . .?'

'Yes, and make sure your arse is fiery red. Now get on with it!'

Anne obeyed: a hundred and fifty times her hand smashed down upon her flesh. She could not hold back her tears, and when she reached the grand total she was surprised to hear herself say haltingly, through her sobs:

'Oh! You have hurt me so badly! How fiery red my flesh feels from the weight of your hand!'

'I love you, Anne,' murmured the Archangel. 'Now, kneel up, arch your back and offer your backside to me – and pleasure yourself with your own hand.'

Anne knelt up and thrust out her buttocks. Her hand slipped between her thighs, where it encountered the open petals of a flower in full bloom. Her first sighs bore testimony to her excitement, and other sighs told her that the Archangel too was becoming more and more aroused. The murmuring intensified, becoming a wailing, a songlike ululation; suddenly the receiver was filled with the voice of the Archangel.

'Come, Anne! Come now!' he was shouting.

Another cry answered his call; Anne was collapsing, racked with tremors, as she drained the last dregs of her ecstasy. She heard a far-off voice murmuring to her out of the abandoned receiver:

'Good night, Anne, my dearest love.'

Then there was silence.

She called her husband back, but there was no answer from the office number. So where was he telephoning from? She never knew. She slid into bed, with a burning backside and a tearful face, and fell asleep – exhausted without feeling satisfied . . .

Standing in between the mirrors, Anne warmed herself with the fires of memory. She unfastened her gown and let it fall at her feet; then looked at herself – dressed as the Archangel liked to see her. A black lace 'waspie' was laced tightly about her waist, lifting up and presenting the globes of her breasts and at the back, thrusting out her naked buttocks. The suspenders, with their gold fastenings, pulled her close-fitting black stockings high up on her thighs. To think of all the whims and fancies she'd had to comply with to satisfy her husband's tastes! One evening last autumn, she had been standing before him, half-naked just as she was today, when he asked:

'Shall we have dinner in Paris?'

Anne hadn't left Septeuil for a month, and she was glad of this chance to escape. She was already climbing the stairs to get ready when the Archangel gave her precise instructions.

'Diamond earrings, long black gloves, and your fur coat,' he ordered.

'And which dress?'

'No dress.'

'What?'

She said no more: that was how the Archangel wanted it to be. She was soon ready. At the bottom of the stairs where he was waiting for her, her husband studied her admiringly. With her perfume, her make-up and that black fur coat which highlighted the snowy brightness of her complexion, she could have been posing for a fashion photograph. But when she opened up her coat to reveal her skimpy underclothes, the shock was a violent one. The Archangel planted a kiss on her gloved hand. At the foot of the steps, he opened the car door for her. The air was chill, and Anne could feel it gnawing at her backside.

The black Bentley was now travelling towards Paris; as they went along the road, the headlights lit up bushes bent and flattened by sudden, cruel gusts of wind. Inside the car, the air was warmed by the heater, and dance music floated gently from the radio. The Archangel held the steering-wheel with one hand, and slipped the other between Anne's thighs. Half-naked in her fur coat, she let herself go completely, trying not to think about the measures she would have to take to avoid being found out in the restaurant they were driving to.

'Anne, use your lips . . .' her husband asked suddenly.

Anne leaned forward, unfastened his flies and exposed his erect penis, which she took into her mouth. The car slowed down and Anne's caresses became bolder; with her gloved hands, she lightly stroked the seed-pods of the fruit she was so patiently tasting. Her kiss became velvet-soft, and her eager tongue made the naked flesh feel as though it were covered in tiny pin-pricks; she took it within her encircling teeth, holding it tight without bruising it. But the Archangel pulled away from her.

'I want to see you. Get out of the car. Stand in front of the headlights and lift up your coat. I saw you like that in a dream one night – half-naked in the wind. Will you do it?'

She replied with a smile.

The car stopped. Anne stationed herself in the light from the headlamps, with her back to the car. She lifted up her fur coat, and the wind lashed at her buttocks. The dance music was still playing on. Afraid that another car might come upon her unawares, Anne took off her coat completely and hurriedly offered the Archangel this surprising picture: tight-waisted in her lace waspie, she turned round on her high heels like a fashion model showing off some indecent outfit. And she gave herself to the night, to the wind that raced across the countryside, to the mechanical, pop-eyed sphinx which the car had become. And she gave herself to the Archangel. Her husband soon called her back: shivering all over, Anne allowed herself to be caressed by his warm hands and lips; and slowly the icy outer

122

casing which had covered her melted away. The dance music was still soothing the pictures passing in procession beneath her closed eyelids when she felt the Archangel lay down between her parted thighs and enter her. He held her face in his hands, and his tongue entered Anne's mouth, stifling her cries.

The restaurant was decked out like an old wine cellar. Anne wrapped her coat tightly about her and went down the staircase. She stumbled on the gravel which covered the floor, and was lucky to reach her table without coming to grief. The waiter invited her to leave her coat in the cloakroom, and the Archangel could not resist a smile when she refused. The women who were sitting at the other tables had bare shoulders and low-necked dresses.

The walls were decorated with miniatures recalling the history of this old district; minstrels sang old folk-songs; the dishes on the menu took their inspiration from medieval recipes. The diners drank mead out of pewter goblets, and a sparkling wine with a magical name: 'vin fou' (the wine of madness).

Anne soon forgot her outlandish outfit: she rolled up her coat sleeves to bare her arms to the elbows, and flung back the collar to free her shoulders. In this way she half-offered herself, but the Archangel imagined how surprised the other diners would be if Anne had suddenly taken off her fur coat.

The table had been chosen deliberately, so that only the Archangel could see his companion, from a certain angle. He asked her to bare one breast, to take it in her hand and present it to him, which she did. Then he told her, confidentially:

'Beneath these vaults, in these cellars which were once prisons, I knew you. You were just as beautiful and even more naked than you are today. I submitted you to a thousand torments, do you remember? All night long you cried out. Do you remember?'

'I remember,' replied Anne, without looking away from the Archangel.

'In that case, scratch your breast with your nails as my nails once scratched it.'

123

Anne, looking straight into the Archangel's eyes, buried her nails in her flesh, dragging four deep red furrows as her nails moved slowly towards the erect bud of her nipple. The pain was acute, and tears shone in her eyes, but she smiled with the corners of her mouth, in that special way which betrayed her inner turmoil. And then, in the Archangel's gaze, she caught sight of the glimmering light which must prevail in Hell, shining on the Lake of Desire – and Anne shivered as she accepted in advance the burning promises of that gaze. And yet the Archangel's conversation was lively. With sharpened wit, he joined her in making fun of the people who surrounded them. A singer came to their table. Accompanying himself on the guitar, he sang an old ballad in which rejected knights tormented a cruel lady:

> 'Tis said that for revenge
> Until the daylight hour
> They used her body basely
> Up there on the high tower.

The Archangel and Anne joined in the chorus, which praised the virtues of the knights, whose names were intoned one by one, like a litany:

> Thibault, Count of Spain
> Gontran de Montigny
> Charles, Duke of Brittany
> And Monsieur de Coucy.

Lulled by the warmth of the wine and the nostalgic songs, Anne drifted away into another world. She visualised herself in a château which was not Septeuil, but Chambord or Chenonceaux. She was indeed naked – not in her fur coat, but beneath a robe of heavy woollen cloth, whose bodice was embroidered in gold thread; and she saw the narrow table suddenly grow longer. She was surrounded by glossy-bearded noblemen; next to her sat her husband, dressed in a black, high-collared doublet edged with white satin. On his fingers sparkled precious stones. He was smiling at her. Watching attentively from the far end of the hall was the Winged Lion, which looked as though it had flown straight out of the tapestry at Septeuil. Anne was trying to find a place for the Unicorn in this fleeting scene when the Archangel's voice called her back from her dream; he had risen to his feet and was smiling at her, suggesting that they should leave.

She was hoping that this evening their lovemaking would be gentle and peaceful, but in the studio flat where they spent the night Anne was tied down and torn to pieces on the bed by an Archangel who had once again become a demon. At dawn, she experienced for the first time the delicious torture of ice cubes sliding over her bruised and battered flesh. She was racked with long bouts of shivering, and these unreal caresses brought tears to her eyes . . .

Moving in this way from one image to another, Anne found tokens of her glory or her misfortune. Some days, she felt haughty and proud that she had suffered so many ordeals: at other times, she saw them as an excuse to feel indignant and to grieve. Coming face to face with the mirrors which reflected the sleek image of her body, she was amazed to see that her ill-treatment had not left any marks. True, there was a very thin scar low down on her belly (the result of the one and only time that the Archangel had used a knife on her), but her husband attached too much importance to her beauty to impair it with wounds. Anne stroked the scar on her belly, casting her mind back to that August night in Spain when the storm had raged about them; the lightning must have struck an electric cable, as the innkeeper had brought candles to light their room. The candle flames lit up the Archangel's face: he was naked and golden, like a bronze statue. Anne let her caressing fingers follow the contours of his torso with its muscular shoulders; the narrowing lines of waist and hip; then felt once again the fullness of his thighs. Her kisses began under the Archangel's arm, tickling his armpit; then they surrounded his shoulders, and landed suddenly on his ear before brushing his belly and finally fastening on his penis. Anne was in the grip of a tremendous fever: she wanted to have the Archangel at her mercy – and he was. No doubt touched by such ardour, he suggested something which he had never offered to any other woman: that they should sanctify their union by mingling their blood. They had brought a dagger back from Toledo – its handle was inlaid with gold and its wafer-thin blade had an edge like a razor. The Archangel made a very fine incision low down on Anne's belly and pressed his lips to it. But when it was Anne's turn to wound him, she panicked. Nevertheless she tried to do it and didn't have the strength to push it further in. So the Archangel had to take her hand himself and push in the dagger: the wound deepened, and there was blood everywhere. Anne lost all control of herself and called for help, drank the blood without stemming the flow – and made such a din that finally the innkeeper was awakened by her cries and entered the room, to be dumbfounded by the sight of Anne – naked and white – kneeling over her husband's belly with her lips pressed to his wound, and presenting her blood-spattered loins to the storm-lit night.

They left the village at first light – only then noticing its name: it was called 'Baiser-de-la-Nuit' (Kiss of Night).

The trip had other surprises to offer them; they saw a woman – her body painted like the moon – dancing in a courtyard in Seville. Her only ornaments were a rose and two fans. Then there was Barcelona, where Anne walked naked under her sun-coloured dress. She crossed squares and bustling boulevards. Beneath the red lights of Bario-Chino, they met the shrill-voiced women with clear complexions and midnight-black eyes; each smile met answering words from unknown lips.

One afternoon, in Ripoll, it was so hot that they were soaked with sweat, so they went into a church to cool down. The darkness of the vaulted ceilings and the threatening gleam from the stained-glass windows unsettled Anne. In a side chapel, an old woman was on her knees, praying before two candles. Further off, they found a windowless apse, deep and round and with all the atmosphere of a tomb. The shadows were moving in the light from a candle.

In the hazy candlelight, Anne made out heavy, violet curtains, which she was sure were hiding skeletons or ghosts. She did not want to lift up the material. The Archangel did so, but so briskly that she wasn't sure that she had seen *something* there in the dark. She felt the heavy air strike her face, confirming her impression: those curtains were hiding *nothing*. Behind them, in unimaginable depths, stretched the dark emptiness of subterranean halls. She shivered with distress and with desire as she imagined the earth sloping down inexorably towards Hell. And then the Archangel came up to her.

'Go into the corner and lift up your dress,' he said softly.

Anne could not hide her surprise: such an act, in this place, would be a sin. The Archangel looked at her: and she could not bear the weight of his gaze. She thought she heard her father's voice, reminding her of the dangers to which we expose ourselves when we sin in the full knowledge of what we are doing: sin then takes on the aspect of defiance. And yet Anne made up her mind to do it, murmuring: Oh well, if God does exist, let Him show Himself today! Let him make the ceilings crumble and rain down stones upon us! A quick glance reassured her that the old woman was still praying; behind her, a monk was lighting candles around a statue.

Anne moved into the dark corner of the apse. The Archangel was ready for pleasure and stood between the curtains. Then she turned round and with a single movement hoisted up her dress, baring her buttocks and her legs.

'Push out your backside,' murmured the Archangel. 'Thrust it out . . .'

Anne thrust out her buttocks and moved them about lewdly. Slowly and at his leisure, the Archangel sated himself. Inside the church, nothing had moved.

When they reached the door, they came upon the monk

127

who had been lighting candles. He nodded to them, respectfully. And so this jealous God, this God whose anger was formidable – or so the priests claimed – had allowed his house to be defiled without doing a thing.

Outside, they spotted a deserted close on the other side of a grille, but Anne could not rid her mind of the memory of that dark vault where she had offered herself to an Archangel as he stood on the threshold of Hell. What tormented cries these old stones must have stifled! As she walked past the darkest of the walls, almost touching them, she thought she could hear the voices of people who had been walled up inside. They were singing canticles though their jaws were knit tight shut and – she imagined in terror – their eye-sockets were stuffed with plaster . . .

Anne stood there in the watery gleam from the mirrors, and shivered. Her daydreams had taken a baneful turn; if she listened any more, she would unearth memories which terrified her: memories of the carnival at Venice, or the Beaune asylum, which she had promised herself she would forget. Fearful of falling prey to their lure, she went back to her room, slid into bed, and – with every light switched off and the sheet pulled up over her eyes – she tried to sing herself to sleep with an old song from her childhood.

The words which she sang softly did not still her fever. She saw the Archangel in the role of judge; he wore an ecclesiastical gown tied with a blood-red sash which increased the sternness of his features. His unyielding voice intoned:

'Anne, I have imprisoned you within the mirrors, and all these reflections will destroy you, for henceforth you shall be your own worst enemy.'

Terrified, Anne began her song again, lingering on each word. After a long struggle she finally fell asleep.

Now, at the bottom of the lake of her memory, crystal angels, sleeping gardens, naked women, water-weeds, all moved away with slow sandy movements, and were lost in forgetfulness.

That night, in her dreams, Anne was to take the royal road which the old man used to talk about: when she awoke, she felt as though she were bathed in light. What voyage had led her to such bright frontiers, and why this particular night? Last night, everything had seemed to be stacked against her. Sadly, she retained no memory of the dreams which had so calmed her.

She got out of bed, ran to the window and to her surprise found that the trees were in blossom and full of birdsong, and a curving water spray was playing over the flowers in the flowerbeds: in short, all the soaring grace of a spring morning. She was so happy that she let her hair down, and unfastened her bodice to let the sun play on her full breasts. She would have liked to run naked in the gardens, to stand under the water spray and feel its caresses, to feel beneath her buttocks the grass's firm, strong lips. How gladly she would have played the serpent today!

She remembered a morning like this when the Archangel had taken her into the gardens. When they were away from the house, and in no danger of being seen, Anne undressed. She was hoping for some new pleasure, but was disappointed when it was described to her. All her husband wanted to do was to film her in different positions. Without being able to explain why, Anne was suspicious of such games: reproducing movement held some kind of magical quality for her, and whilst she enjoyed films featuring actors she did not know, she could not bear to see herself on a screen. Perhaps the Archangel wanted to force her into this division of the self which was so painful to her? That is what she thought at first, but when he showed her the positions, she realised that her husband would derive pleasure simply from watching them.

What she had to do was bend towards the ground, with her copper-coloured hair hanging down over her breasts, and offer up her soft, open buttocks to the indiscreet lens. And then the Archangel wanted to see her lie down, like a beautiful marble statue on the watery green of the grass, and she had to lift her legs slowly to give the fullest view of the rosy blooms of her sex. After that, she had to bring her naked breasts close to the camera, show them from different angles to demonstrate their firmness, and then cover them with her beautiful hands to show their size. Her fingers toyed with the pink, erect nipples, kneading the flesh; then she was made to kneel down, with her arms raised above her head, and bend over backwards. For a long time, her parted breasts pointed heavenwards.

The next scene was more tranquil. At the far end of the gardens, a stream murmured under the trees. Anne bathed in it, playing with the sunlit drops of water – a modern-day nymph whose laughter and supple grace were captured by the camera.

The adventure took a different turn that evening, when the Archangel showed Anne the film sequence. Her first reaction was surprise when she saw the colours: her snowy-white flesh, her red hair, and the pink tips of her breasts took on a startling brilliance against the background of greenery. But some of the poses were even more indecent than she had feared! The lens had taken ever-closer shots of her backside – so close, in fact, that the last shot filled the entire screen and revealed every secret detail of her flesh. The Archangel sat beside her whilst the film was running. He took hold of her hand and Anne was obliged to caress him whilst he said to her:

'Look at what you're thrusting at me! That's what I see when you offer your arse to me. Can you imagine anything more indecent?'

Anne moaned in distress. 'No, Anne,' he consoled her. 'You're the most beautiful and the most modest of women, and if I have often enjoyed looking at you, it was because I knew how painful it was for you to pose like that. In the end you came to enjoy it, but at first you had to overcome your better nature . . .' Anne had to agree with him. 'And so,' the Archangel continued, quietly, 'your pleasure was all the more extreme because you knew that it was a guilty pleasure. For after all, it's a sin to offer yourself even to your husband in the way you're doing – look: doggy-fashion, like a bitch!' The Archangel had grabbed hold of her, and was forcing her to watch the screen though she tried to turn her eyes away. Anne resisted him, but he laid her across his knees, lifted up her dress, raised his hand and brought it down upon her naked flesh. Anne cried out, begged him for mercy, tried to get away – but all in vain. The Archangel was enjoying the double pleasure of watching the pictures at the same time as punishing her, and he did not stop until the film ended. When it was over, he treated his beautiful wife with genuine tenderness – caressing her, drying her tears, begging for her forgiveness and winning it at the very moment when he sent her into a new paroxysm of pleasure . . .

Standing naked in the sunshine, Anne shivered. The flowers and birdsong had drawn her out onto the balcony, but the first memory she had indulged in had plunged her soul back into darkness: the gardens seemed less joyful, and the early-morning brightness more fragile. Last night's sufferings, which she had thought were wiped out for good, would never be over. She realised that she must occupy her mind and set out a detailed timetable for her day.

Whenever the Archangel was at the château, Anne didn't have a moment to herself: there was a constant succession of new duties to perform to satisfy the demands of her husband's pleasure. When he wasn't at home, she had to invent tasks to try to stave off boredom. The servant, Jorg, freed her from all the household chores, and although she gave her orders and saw that they were carried out, and sometimes passed the time of day with the gardener, she soon found herself alone again. For several months, Anne applied herself to music. She practised piano exercises conscientiously and ended up being able to play little pieces she didn't like – badly. After that, she dabbled in painting: skimming her shaky brush over canvases she could never finish. Finally, she tried to go back to the books which had brought light into her adolescent years. She knew that the rules laid down in these books were true and just, but – since she had made up her mind not to follow them – her reading programme lost its purpose, and she gave it up.

From that point, the poisonous flowers of melancholy began to grow within her heart. A fatal attraction pushed her towards that last refuse of the lonely: the recollection of the past. Nowadays, memories of long-dead joys and the contemplation of her own beauty were her only pleasures.

This conclusion deterred her from making the effort she wanted to make. Why bother trying to occupy my time? she thought. Nothing will free me from myself. Only the Archangel can do that. And so, drained of strength and of desire, she got dressed and went down into the gardens.

A yellow and grey bird flew down onto the sandy garden path. Anne stopped, and the bird lifted his glossy little head, opened his beak, and two musical trills rose up from his pretty throat. Then, pleased with himself, he puffed out his feathers and fled. Anne smiled. The simple joys which surrounded her, all the sounds of this winged world, took her mind back to a scene last spring: the gardens at Versailles, where the Archangel had taken her one morning.

Just like today, the birds were singing: singing out brightly and lustily, to show how busy they were. Many nests were built that morning in the trees at Versailles! The gardens were deserted and spring had caught the Archangel's imagination. He opened his coat to reveal a little twig which soon became a slender branch, and then – in Anne's hand – grew into a great, thick, knotted bough, swollen with sap. And so he stood there in the sunshine, caressed by a silent woman whose beautiful face betrayed no knowledge of what her hand was doing.

The Archangel decided that he wanted to play a little game: he would pretend to be a passer-by who didn't know Anne. He asked her to pull her dress right up to the tops of her legs as he came up to her, and then to part them. She agreed to play along. The Archangel went some distance away and then came back towards the bench where Anne was sitting. He experienced an extraordinary degree of pleasure at the moment when she uncovered her long legs, then her stocking-tops and the snowy brightness of her thighs, and finally those rosy pearls in their fur-lined casket. Anne had displayed herself with indifference, as he had asked her to, and played her part so well that she really believed she had aroused a stranger; that added spice to the little charade, which was no doubt why she was harking back to it today.

She cast a glance about her: there was no gardener and no Jorg to benefit from the sight if she had taken it into her mind to display herself to them. Alone in the midst of the flowers, as she was when she stood in front of the mirrors, Anne felt as though she could come to life only through the Archangel.

'The hand caresses, but so does the eye . . .' he had told her one day. 'If I were blind, I could no longer love you. To enjoy coupling with you, I must first excite my mind by evoking some image of you; and so, with these mirrors, I hold you imprisoned in promises of pleasure . . .'

For a moment, she dreamed of all the different outfits and settings in which he had liked to take her. One winter, in Austria, he took her a long way from the hotel to a frozen lake. There, he made her undress and put on her skates: the white, calf-length boots were her only ornament. Anne enjoyed dancing on the ice; light-footed, she pirouetted, jumped, and traced and retraced figures on the ice. The Archangel watched her from the bank, admiring the backward thrust of her buttocks, which shook as she moved, and the sudden surprise of her breasts, which disappeared and reappeared with the rhythm of each turn. The cold air had brought colour to her complexion, and she became a beautiful pink snow-statue, exciting the wind's curiosity in the sparkling morning, in the silence of the white lake and the white forest. There in the sunshine, she danced for him alone, as the trees cast their frozen lace border around her.

One foggy November morning in Paris, when they were driving slowly across the Bois, with the car headlamps on, the Archangel wanted to see her stand outside, close to the windscreen, and caress herself. Anne got out of the car.

The tree-lined avenue was invisible in the mist. She could see no one (though she heard footsteps around her), but the fear of being discovered made her heart beat faster. The Archangel sat at the steering-wheel and watched her. She unbuttoned her coat, lifted up her dress, bared her belly and – parting her love-lips with her finger – caressed her clitoris. The Archangel saw her through the dwindling clear patch on the windscreen and for a long time he mused upon this unreal, bare-thighed woman standing in the fog, exactly as though she were a dream-image which with each breath on the glass drew farther away.

One April day – here at Septeuil – the rain had spent the whole morning spreading its veil over the gardens. In the gap between two showers, the Archangel wanted to go out. So Anne put on her boots, covered her hair with a scarf and completed this scanty outfit with a white, transparent raincoat. She took a long walk on the grass. The Archangel followed her, in silence. He watched her scarcely-covered buttocks moving, and when Anne turned towards him, was assailed by the twin delights of her breasts and the shadowy triangle of her belly. That day, they went back home without his having touched her, but that evening, by the fireside, his desire was ferocious.

The Archangel did not only like to look at her: he also liked to show her off. One afternoon, in their bedroom, Anne was submitting to his caresses when he announced:

'A friend of mine is in the next room. He's watching you. Don't turn round – you'll see him downstairs shortly.'

The Archangel made her shake herself, and with kisses and slaps made her backside and her bosom dance to his tune. Anne caught sight of the open door, but saw no one, and yet, at the moment of her orgasm she heard a low groan coming from the next room.

At teatime, the friend arrived as promised. He bowed to Anne respectfully, and there was nothing in his behaviour to suggest that he had just seen her moaning and naked. But her husband's expression maintained the ambiguity of the situation, and she never found out how much this man knew about her.

... The sunlight was burning her eyelids, and Anne opened her eyes ... In the grip of memory, she had stretched herself out in the grass without realising it. Her pink linen dress was tight at the waist and flared out in folds over her hips; where the bodice fastened, it revealed the furrow between her breasts. She hitched her skirt up onto her thighs, pointed her toe inside her dainty shoe, and lifted it up to see it shine in the sun. The warmth was so sweet that she pulled her dress higher up; the sunshine caressed her, and her thighs moved apart. Her perfume – reminiscent of sandalwood – wafted up from her warm skin. She lifted up her head, let down her hair and its shining waves tumbled down over her shoulders. And then, surrendering herself completely to the caresses of sun, wind and grass, the lovely Anne fell asleep.

She was hoping that this trick would allow her to stop thinking, and that the light-heartedness of her surroundings would enter her dreams. But it was not to be: as soon as she began to dream, her torments began again.

She saw herself lying naked on paving stones in the darkness and the cold. Where was she? Could it be a church? She heard the amplified sound of heels striking the ground, and the long, faraway echo of a door opening. Suddenly the Archangel appeared. He was standing over her; and she could see the whole of his face, bathed in the whites of light. His voice, as he questioned her, was soft – and yet in this vaulted cell it took on a disturbing resonance.

'Anne, do you know why you are here?'

'I do,' said Anne.

And immediately she was seized with panic, trying to understand what crime she could have committed. But the Archangel persisted in his questions.

'Will you therefore pronounce in your own words the accusation which is levelled against you?'

'I stand accused of betraying my father's teachings.'

'And you shall see!' screeched the Archangel. 'You shall see just how much your betrayal has offended him!'

And then Anne saw the old man's stiff corpse rise up

from the ground, as though someone were lifting the lid of a tomb with its stone effigy still attached to it. He was wearing the same suit he had on the day he died. The Archangel had moved away to one side, and Anne could now see nothing but her father. At first, she glimpsed his face through a sort of fog: she could not make out his features, only the shape of his head, the white patch that represented his hair ... All at once, as though drawn out from the shadows by a brilliant light, the outline loomed into focus and Anne screamed in fear and revulsion. Leprous skin, a death's-head grin and staring eyes had turned her father's face into a mask of terror. Death – for that is what this spectre was – was now bending over Anne. Screaming, she tried to escape its avid kiss, but felt its cold lips and corpse's teeth enter her mouth, and her stomach heaved at the taste of earth and rotting flesh. When Anne came to her senses, the apparition had disappeared; only the Archangel remained, watching her. 'Tell me – do you regret the crime you have committed?' He cried out suddenly.

'Yes,' wailed Anne, 'yes, yes ...' and she heard the thin sound floating away into the echoing vaults.

'You lie!' screeched the Archangel, 'you regret nothing – for at this very moment you are lying in the meadow at Septeuil, you are sleeping in the sunshine and hoping that when you wake you will find me beside you!'

'Yes, that's true,' Anne said to herself. 'I'm sleeping in the meadow, and all of this is only a dream,' and her distress melted away when the Archangel began to speak again. This time his voice was louder.

'You are waiting for me, and you hope that in your dreams you will encounter the image of me which you love. Admit it: your only desire is to pander to my vices!'

'I admit it,' said Anne, who was writhing about on the pavement as though the Archangel were caressing her.

'In that case, I shall satisfy you!'

The Archangel wrenched Anne's legs apart and the whip's first stroke landed upon her parted love-lips. Anne expected to feel it bite; but as the blow fell a sweet sensation of warmth spread through her loins, as though he was flaying her with thongs of velvet; each successive stroke shook her composure, aroused her pleasure, and she began to moan.

She was in such a state of arousal that she woke up – and yet she could still feel the insistent strokes between her thighs. Lifting up her head, she was amazed to see her own hand between her legs, stroking herself. Trembling, she brought herself to orgasm.

The shower-spray covered Anne with its cloak of pins and needles: she rubbed her skin with an abrasive washing-mitt, douched herself with harsh disinfectants which burned her as they washed away the impurities. When her flesh was stinging and her skin was white as snow, she covered her arms and breasts with perfume, and stepped into a close-fitting dress which she pulled up so that she could put on the lace suspender-belt to hold up her stockings. Once she had put on her stockings and polished shoes, and combed her hair until it shone, she felt she was ready to receive the Archangel – should he condescend to come back. The pink dress was lying on the bed where she had thrown it. It still bore traces of the grass. Anne flung it into the grate and stirred up the fire.

At the top of the house there was a long loft, which was used for drying fruit and as a lumber room. It was piled to the ceiling with broken lanterns, mirrors and antiquated weapons: the books were inside an old trunk.

Anne sat down close to a window, the sunlight illuminating a notebook she had just discovered which she was holding on her knee. Her father had scrawled across a few pages, and his notes were a revelation to Anne. At first, she thought she was reading a fictional story whose hero was not the person who was writing it:

A rope was placed in my hand: a rope which was to lead me towards the light – but I exchanged the stout, honest hemp for the Devil's fine thread, and now each step I take brings me closer to Hell.

How could the old man have known such torments – this old man, whose fair gaze, high forehead and calm features looked out at her from an old photograph she had rediscovered? What sins could he be guilty of? Anne found her answer when she turned the page.

What is the use of finding the right road, if I don't want to follow it? I envy you, my blind brother, ministering to your own passions without realising that they are sinful! The only happy man is the man who does not hear the voice of the Angel within him. Is there any more terrible curse than that of preferring a turgid bog to water trickling by beneath the palm trees? You know that the true source is there, and you know the route you have to take to get to it across the sand, yet you're afraid of confronting the desert. And so I deceived my thirst with earthly waters, all the time pining for the never-failing spring. What an unhappy day it was when I was shown the path to the oasis! What's the use of wanting to progress towards heaven? Everything confines me down here: Anne and her beautiful, magical body, her mother Isis whom I take by force every night. Her cries and her tears are much sweeter music to my ears than the song of the Angels, and yet my pleasures are poisoned, tainted! How could I ever hope to experience peace? Fuelled by my own weaknesses, I find new zest in them even as I repent giving in to them. And so my soul is a confusion of remorse and desire, one serving to fuel the other.

Tonight, as I have done so many nights before, I am waiting in the room next to Anne's, peeping through the spy-hole in the hope of seeing her undress. This child has so many charms already, that a beautiful fruit must surely spring forth from so many flowers! With her, I should like to achieve all that I have failed in myself; to teach her to drink the clear water and to shine in the sun. Is it wicked to deceive her about my own character, to play for her benefit a part which I could not sustain before God? I pray that she will forgive me when she discovers my secret. I have loved her so well! I wanted to give her the weapons to resist ill-omened beings – beings like myself! And what have I given to my

poor Isis? My only pleasure has been to see her chastised.
So why is it that I have no desire to force myself upon
Anne, even though she is so beautiful, and her flawless flesh
invites my blows even more compellingly? Perhaps this is
the only ray of light left in my soul? At the chosen hour, I
must settle my account – and I am ready to do so, even
though I know better than anyone what that act will mean
for me. But Anne's judgement matters more to me. This
evening – as though I deserved it – I consoled myself with
this thought: 'I demand nothing from my precious child but
smiles.'

Anne read no more. She gazed out at the countryside without seeing it, and felt tears flowing down her cheeks. How
much tenderness she felt for the old man; how well she
understood his sufferings, which were also hers! Those lines
had provided the explanation she was seeking: if she had
surrendered herself to the Archangel, it was because she
was fated by blood to be a captive, destined like her
mother Isis to find all her pleasures in servitude. Her
father's efforts could do nothing for her: the Archangel had
given her back her true self. And her true place was here,
in this lonely château where she had felt the whip's lash
and played the slave to a tyrant! From now on, she would
await his return steadfastly, always beautiful and groomed,
as naked as he could wish her to be, ready for each act of
indecency and even instigating it! How cheerfully she could
now rise above her woes! In her bedroom, she would set
out all the instruments of torture, so that the Archangel
would lay eyes on them instantly. She would devise new,
untried games and would bring her cousin Henriette to the
château from the provinces where she was kicking her
heels. Henriette was only sixteen, but already good enough
to eat, and she could awaken the Archangel's lust: Anne
would join her in satisfying all her husband's passions! Her
mind was in a fever of excitement. Rushing downstairs into
the hall, she met Jorg who was waiting for her there with
a letter in his hand.

Once she was back in her room, Anne had to read the

Archangel's message several times before she understood what was happening to her.

Anne, he wrote, *I love you and yet you will not see me again. For me, you branded love with your image, and yet these dark joys lacked the sunlight of happiness. That is what I am going away to look for, a long way from here. I am leaving you what I own, and Septeuil is now in your name. Understand me: you will always be my accomplice, my queen. I am not leaving you, my most beautiful of women – I am tearing myself from your arms as though you were a red-hot fire about to consume me, and by this act I give you back to life. If on my journey I do not find what I am looking for, I shall come back to Septeuil. Perhaps I shall find the house empty, but if you have waited for me, you will find me at your mercy. If I am never to see you again, I leave you to whomsoever you happen to meet. He will love you – undoubtedly less, but, alas, better than your dark 'Archangel'.*

Anne sat there like a statue until dusk fell, silently burning, as though she were run through with daggers. When the darkness was complete, she wished that she could die – it seemed as though she might simply fade away with the daylight, effortlessly. The gleam of the night's first stars filtered through her tears – perhaps their flickering light was a sign? Perhaps the old man and Isis were calling to her to join them there in the empty sky! But straight away she felt the Archangel's words burning within her: '*If on my journey I do not find what I am looking for, I shall come back to Septeuil. I shall come back to Septeuil. I shall come back to Septeuil . . .*' How could she run away? How could she think of dying, as long as he still lived? Perhaps if she had enough love and patience she could hope that one day everything would be given back to her? She wanted to turn that hope into certainty, and got ready to spend the night as the Archangel would have wished, had he been there. She made up her face, selected her dark blue negligée, slipped on her shoes and, perfumed, painted, and naked under her thin covering, she went into the hall of mirrors.

Anne stood under the chandeliers, in the carpet's sea of red, and looked questioningly at her reflection: this creature dreamed up by a mad angel – her diamond jewellery concealing a wound that gaped wide with every heartbeat. Why bother to give her such extraordinary charms when all she needed was to be naked and defiled?

She walked towards the fire. Flames were licking around the bark on the logs, which whined piteously as they curled and buckled amid the glowing coals. Anne was hypnotised as she watched them writhe, wreathed in scarlet. As though in a dream, she unfastened her gown. Guided by an invisible hand, she took down a braided whip from the wall and stroked it across her breasts. This was her true image, the image which the Archangel had given to her! Turning her back on the flames, she thrust out her backside and landed a first blow upon this flesh which had aroused so many desires. And Anne whipped herself into a frenzy of sensual pleasure – not realising that the Archangel was not coming back.

If you're passing through Septeuil, don't try to find the castle – it's inaccessible. And even if you were unlucky enough to discover the building, there would be no point in ringing the doorbell: Jorg has his orders, and he won't let you in. But you might just see light shining through an open window. You will not see her, but if you draw very near you will hear the lovely Anne moaning, and tearing at her own flesh, and you will surely think it a great pity that the hard-hearted Archangel hasn't condescended to return.

But why should be come back? He knew that the forces which he had liberated would for ever more hold Anne prisoner. Three forces – three demons which served him unquestioningly, throughout this tale. Blood, mirrors, and the night.

141

An Education in Charme

I was in the middle of my eighteenth-birthday celebrations at Mme Hartmann's finishing-school in Vevey when the headmistress came and told me that my parents had been killed in an accident.

I spent the next few days in the depths of despair. Then a cousin of my mother's came to take me to the estate where her family were waiting for me: my cousins Véronique and Lucile, and my aunt Clara. I had always been fascinated by their château's name. 'Next summer, we're going to Charme,' my mother used to say. And immediately, in my mind's eye, I would see the gardens and their trees filled with birdsong. My uncle Frédéric – a handsome man of forty-five – told me about his wife. I remembered her; with her white skin, red hair and slender waist. Clara was said to be the prettiest woman in our family. And she was certainly the most elegant, for the life which my parents' cousins led at Charme was one big social whirl, which – people said – had contributed to their success.

The fact that my schoolfriends were always telling me what a splendid body I had hadn't made any impression on me: as soon as I saw my cousins I knew that they were much more beautiful, and more elegant too; and although Véronique was the same age as I and Lucile was only a year older, both girls already had all the confident poise of young women. They seemed happy to be spending the holidays with me.

My aunt had given me a room near to her own. A few hours after I arrived, she came into my room, carrying a large cardboard box which she put down on the bed.

'You haven't had time to find mourning clothes suitable for the time of year. Here are some. They're your size. Go on – try them on.'

After my bath, I looked at my reflection in a big mirror and was not pleased: I felt I was too plump, and too pale; I sucked in my cheeks to make my face look thinner. But there was nothing I could do to reduce the jaunty thrust of my breasts, nor the ample, weighty curve of my backside.

I was just pulling my bra-straps onto my shoulders when my aunt came back.

'Darling, at your age you don't need any support. Follow the example of your cousins, who model themselves on me.

She opened her bodice, to reveal her naked bosom.

'Come here, and I'll explain . . .'

We stood together, bare-breasted, in front of the mirror, and compared the firmness of our breasts. Clara placed her hand on mine, asking me to judge whether or not her own had lost any of their elasticity. When I felt the weight of these fleshy fruits in my hand, I was filled with the desire to brush their crests with my lips, to sink my teeth into their plumpness. As I stood there, looking at my reflection, I could not stop myself saying why it made me sad.

'My bosom is too big. And it's nothing compared with the rest of me . . .'

My aunt bade me turn round so that my backside was facing the mirror. I looked over my shoulder at that ball of white flesh, perched high on my thighs, whilst Clare murmured dreamily:

'It's true – you do have an enormous Montespan.'

Seeing I was surprised, she led me to a picture showing a naked lady, lying on her side on a bed.

'As you can see, at her birth the Marquise de Montespan was endowed with the most beautiful example of her century. And so, as a mark of esteem, we have given her name to that part of our bodies. And this is another part of you which has no need of clothing. For centuries, women wore nothing, and – whilst fashion may have shortened our skirts – decency did not demand that we should be forced to wear knickers: far from hiding the body, they reveal it. Like my daughters, you will have no need of them.'

'But Auntie,' I ventured, 'isn't that indecent?'

'You think so? Just look.'

Aunt Clara turned round, pinched up her skirt on either side and lifted it, uncovering a plump, white backside which – at the time – seemed completely indecent to me. I felt myself blushing violently, and felt silly standing there naked, a swollen lump of flesh. Without saying anything else, I hurriedly put on my black stockings, attached them to the suspenders, and covered myself with my underskirt; the crêpe fabric of my dress was fitted close to my breasts and my hips, and the cardboard box also contained a pair of high-heeled court shoes.

Perched on my high heels, I looked in the mirror at my lengthened silhouette.

'You look like a French maid in an operetta,' Clara told me, laughing. 'Black suits you. Come here, and I'll do your hair.'

Were my aunt's hands endowed with strange powers? Her hands slid over my hair and then started to massage me. Shivers began to spread through my whole body.

'Little beauty,' she murmured. 'How happy I am to have you with us!'

She put some of her lipstick on my lips. Then, feeling curiously as though I had aged ten years in a few minutes, I followed her down to the drawing-room where Lucile, Véronique and uncle Fred were waiting for us so we could all go in to dinner.

The meal was very jolly, and I was complimented on my dress, my hairstyle and my complexion. I realised that, as I spoke, I was looking at my cousins' bodices and trying to make out the shape of their breasts under the material, and imagining their backsides as free as my aunt's rounded arse. I blushed at the thought that my uncle knew this family tradition, and perhaps knew that I had already fallen in with it.

'Is anything wrong?' asked Véronique.

'Sylvia isn't used to being naked under her dress yet,'

replied Lucile with a pretty little laugh. 'At first, you feel the air moving about all over you.'

And I did indeed feel the cold running icy fingers over my thighs. Luckily, the conversation moved on to another topic; when the meal was over, I cherished the hope that no one would take any more notice of me for the rest of the evening. However, the surprises were not over for me yet.

When we were in the drawing-room and coffee had been served, uncle Fred said calmly:

'We've got an account to settle – isn't that so, Lucile?'

'Oh no! Not this evening. Not in front of Sylvia!'

'Sylvia is a member of the family, so she should know our customs. Now: what should you expect as your punishment?'

'To see my Montespan wear cardinal purple.'

'And who do you choose to perform this ceremony?'

Lucile had a malicious gleam in her eyes.

'I choose Sylvia,' she said.

My aunt invited me to sit down on the sofa. Lucile came across of her own free will, lay down across my knees and advised me in conspiratorial tones:

'Not too hard. I'll do the same for you some time.'

Before I had had time to understand what she was talking about, my cousin had lifted up her dress to reveal a white, dense rump, neatly divided into two by a thin line the colour of tea-roses.

'Well, what are you waiting for?' asked my aunt. 'Your cousin's Montespan demands its cardinal purple robe.'

Instinctively, I put my arms around Lucile's shoulders and put my weight upon them, so hard that her beautiful backside spread out across my knees like a water-lily. I raised my right arm and my hand fell back down into the midst of her buttocks, leaving a red mark. Lucile gave a faint cry. Breathless, I raised my arm again, and was overwhelmed by a growing desire to see all this mass of flesh covered in flaming red. The more I hit her, the more the sound of the blows transformed my state of mind. Not until my burning hand gave way could I stop. Lucile rolled onto the ground, her hands clasped to her crimson and purple Montespan. Upset by all these emotions, I burst into tears.

My aunt came to my rescue. As she spoke softly to me, I understood that I had to get rid of a tendency to useless emotion, as my cousins had already done: they had long been freed of all sentimentality by the special education which they received from their parents. But was I yet ready to understand it? Poised between curiosity and shame, my body felt suddenly weary and listless, and I was no longer myself. I let my hand rest on Clara's shoulder. My bosom was heaving with sobs, and felt as though it were on fire.

My aunt was kind enough to come to my assistance. She unbuttoned my bodice and pushed back the dress from my breasts, allowing their fat, jolly snouts to spring into view. She placed her hand upon them and began to massage them with the same circular movement which I remembered had been used by the masseuse my poor mother had once sent me to in the hope of slimming me down. My breathing became more regular, I became more able to think clearly, and my flesh became calm once again. Then I opened my eyes. They must have been round with astonishment, for Véronique and Lucile burst out laughing. After looking at the object which had caused my surprise, aunt Clara said to me:

'It's nothing, darling – only Papa Boquet.'

'Papa Boquet?'

'Come here.'

I tried to hide my bosom.

'No, Sylvia, no. Your breasts need fresh air, after all that emotion.'

Then aunt Clara led me away – blushing, hair falling down, tottering on the heels which were too high for me, and preceded by my breasts which looked even whiter and harder against the black dress which squeezed them together. She dragged me towards uncle Fred, leaned over him and invited me to lean over too in order to take a closer look at a skin-covered baton, twenty centimetres long and seven to ten centimetres in circumference. At its end, it wore a pointed cap in a pretty shade of pink, pierced by a little oval opening. Underneath this baton were two big walnuts carried in a double sack of dark skin, which intrigued me enormously.

'This toy looks like an upside-down cup-and-ball game – a "bilboquet". It belongs to your cousins' father, which is why we have given it the family name of Papa Boquet.'

'And what do you do to play with it?'

I heard uncle Fred's deep voice, murmuring:

'She really is charming . . .'

'Well, first of all you kiss it,' went on my aunt. 'You'll see how. Lucile!'

My cousin knelt down in front of her father. I saw her pretty lips part and she swallowed down Papa Boquet right up to the hilt. But then she choked, and her eyes filled with tears. She let go of the toy to get her breath back.

'Silly girl!' shouted my aunt. 'Véronique come here and give your sister twenty slaps!'

Véronique came over and lifted up Lucile, who asked for forgiveness. Twenty resounding slaps fell onto her already-reddened Montespan. My cousin's thighs opened, and she kicked about with her heels: I caught sight of a pink, shining scallop-shell between her legs, and once again I felt the desire to give her a kiss.

When the punishment was over, Véronique sat down on the carpet, but unlike her sister, she began by giving Papa Boquet a series of little licks. This practice must have something to recommend it, because I heard my uncle encouraging his daughter with sighs and my aunt giving her advice. She leaned over, watching to see how her eldest daughter discharged her duties; just as my poor mother once leaned over me, watching how I rolled out pastry, in the days when she was teaching me to cook.

'Now the ring of Anubis,' specified my aunt.

Véronique's lips left the wrinkled double pouch. My cousin bent her head forward and opened her mouth wide. Was she going to try to swallow Papa Boquet whole? No, she closed her jaws gently along the length of the baton. It reminded me of my Vaudois friend Elise Grottwald, and the way I used to make her laugh when I took whole ears of corn into my mouth. So there it was: the baton was caught within the ring formed by those pretty canine teeth – which were, however, rather less dangerous than the fangs of Anubis.

Care had to be taken with this part of the game. With closed eyes, Véronique let go with her teeth and licked the stalk to moisten it, then once again tightened the ring round the body of the baton itself. Deeming the pink cap worthy of special attention, she took a lock of her hair between her fingers and ran it across the round head of Papa Boquet. Because of where I was standing, I was the first to notice a white bead, like a teardrop, appearing at the opening to this marvellous plaything, and I brought it to the attention of the others. Uncle Fred was amused by my surprise. Then aunt Clara called a halt to her daughter's efforts, saying:

'Now we're going to put Papa Boquet in Sylvia's snowy eiderdown.'

Thanks to my aunt's friendly demonstrations, I felt I was now ready to do whatever I was told, and yet I felt slightly uneasy as I lay down on the sofa. My aunt propped up my head with the aid of a cushion and I saw uncle Fred kneel down over me, so that Papa Boquet – which now seemed to be attached to my uncle's body, though I had at first thought he had placed it between his legs for convenience – Papa Boquet slipped in between my breasts; its pink head came up against my lips and caressed them. I did as I was asked, squeezing my breasts together, so as to cover the entire stem of the plaything.

My poor mother, who used to be delighted by my serious attitude to study, would have been happy that day to see how much benefit I was deriving from my cousins' first teachings.

At first, I put up with Papa Boquet's movements as I squeezed it between my breasts, and the way its head bumped against my teeth and my tongue. But I was powerless to resist when – opening my mouth as I had seen the others do – the toy plunged forwards into my throat and threatened to choke me. A wave of nausea overpowered me. Far from extricating itself, the object insisted on pushing itself further in. The only way I could get rid of it was to bite it – which made my uncle cry out.

I had now got to my feet and rebuttoned my dress, and I was plucking up the courage to say that this was quite enough for my first evening, and I'd be obliged if we could call it a day; my uncle looked angry to me. Aunt Clara was standing next to him, looking at me reproachfully.

'Stupid girl! You nearly hurt Frédéric. Seize her, girls, and make her Montespan purple!'

Before I could say a word, my cousins grabbed me and turned me towards the sofa, pulling my arms over the back and tying my wrists together. I pleaded, threatened and kicked out to stop anyone coming near me, but I soon felt each of my thighs being manhandled and irresistibly pulled towards the back of the sofa, to which they were then tied. I was now completely helpless – even more so when my dress and underskirt were thrown over my head. I felt my backside exposed to view, and a hand stroking it. A voice murmured:

'This child has a magnificent Montespan.'

And then a torrent of fire rained down on my nether cheeks. I wriggled about in my bonds, and tried to crouch down, but a blow sent me leaping up again, and the pain made my backside jump up and down like a water-flea. I tried to make out how I was being beaten, and realised that three people were raining down several hundred blows with a cat-o'-nine-tails on my buttocks – sometimes taking turns, and sometimes simultaneously! By the time I was untied, I had fainted away.

My aunt was the first to bring me round. She took me in her arms and, as she calmed my sobs, I felt her unfastening my dress and sliding it down onto my hips. In short, she was undressing me in the middle of the drawing-room ... All I cared about was my burning flesh, and I let her get on with it. I stood in front of a mirror and saw my tear-swollen face, my hard white breasts, my long black stockings and – when I was made to turn round – the dark-red, striped, puffed-up ball of flesh which seemed to me to have doubled in volume and in weight. This sight made me even more distressed.

'Being whipped is nothing, little beauty,' my aunt consoled me. 'Everything that happens to you from now on will be pleasurable. I shall prove it to you. Lean back against the mirror – the coolness will calm you down.'

I obeyed. My aunt kneeled down in front of uncle Fred, and covered handsome Papa Boquet with kisses. This strange plaything suddenly began to jerk about, and plunged right down my aunt's throat, just as it had done with mine. But she was more experienced, and knew how to keep it in her mouth. I even saw her sucking in her cheeks like I used to do at Vevey when I emptied a glass of mint cordial with a straw – though this beverage never made me sigh like my aunt made uncle Fred do. When she put a cambric handkerchief to her lips, I noticed that the plaything was looking rather downcast. Véronique took it in her hand, just as delicately as my schoolfriends and I used to pick up little birds that had fallen out of their nests in the school garden – mind you, we didn't see them grow in our hands like Papa Boquet did. Lucile looked at her father mischievously.

'Put Papa Boquet in Josephine.'

Uncle Fred invited his wife to sit down on the sofa. It was covered in a delectable Trianon blue silk which showed – if there was any need for proof – that aunt Clara had exquisite taste. She leaned against the back, lifted up her long legs and, sliding a hand behind each knee, succeeded in holding them up whilst Papa Boquet burrowed into a fringed jewel-casket. I understood the name which Véronique had given to this family game when uncle Fred placed his fist in the small of his back and slid the fingers of his other hand between the buttons of his waistcoat. The sweet sighs wrung from his wife were punctuated by my cousins shouting:

'Lodi! Montmirail! Arcole! Jena! Austerlitz! Eylau! Berthier! Murat! Kleber!'

And so I was given an opportunity to measure the extent of my good fortune: from now on, I was to belong to a family which knew a charming way to commemorate the heroes of our history.

After this part of the game, aunt Clara said to her elder daughter:

'We're short of a cardinal, my dear. Would you like Sylvia to take care of it, or would you prefer it to be your father?'

'Oh no, I'd prefer Sylvia.'

'You shall make her fly the red flag of October.'

Uncle Fred pulled a cord which made an enormous chandelier come down from the ceiling, and my aunt tied her daughter's wrists to it; when Véronique had taken her dress off, the head of the family handed me a cat-o'-nine-tails and said:

'Only beat her on her Montespan, and do it in your own time.'

Véronique looked at me. I looked in admiration at her streamlined body with its pert breasts and curving backside. I let fly with the first stroke, not too hard.

'Lenin!' chorused uncle Fred, my aunt and Lucile.

The second stroke landed on her.

'Trotsky!' the voices murmured, and several other famous names followed in sequence.

'Stalin! Beria! Mikoyan!'

Véronique's body was covered in red marks. As the chandelier moved from right to left so her body swayed with it, and it really did evoke the picture of a flag blown by the October wind, on a day of revolution! At the twentieth blow, everyone shouted:

'Marx!'

And my uncle said:

'Finished.'

Véronique turned her tear-moistened face towards me and murmured between sobs:

'Thank you, Comrade.'

'And now,' my uncle concluded, 'it's time we were all in bed!'

My aunt came into my room and had a little chat with me:

'As you have seen, dear Sylvia, our family games are simple and honest. Your uncle has the good taste to vary them from one week to the next. Only Sunday evenings are taken up with our games – on the other days we each choose our own pleasures or pastimes. You shall share them with your cousins. You will go dancing and swimming, and horseriding in the forest. My daughters have friends of their own age: one of the boys may make a good match for you one day. You should understand that the aim of our weekly games is to educate our daughters and yourself, so that you may become perfect wives. What's more, we want to show you that the pleasures of the senses are a necessary part of a balanced existence, provided that they are not abused. Since your cousins' needs are gratified once a week (please note that they are virgins and they will remain so) they do not suffer from any bothersome curiosity. Finally, as your uncle is careful to vary the subjects of our games, our little playlets have a different subject every week. This evening it was history, another day it will be Latin, geography or even physics. So you see, we have found a new way of teaching the classical curriculum; and our daughters benefit from it. Tomorrow, we shall organise a picnic in the forest. We shall go there by bicycle and if the weather is fine, we shall enjoy the exercise.'

After these words, which allowed me a glimpse of singularly fulfilling holidays to come, my dear aunt kissed me and turned off the light.

As I snuggled down in my bed, my heart was filled with gratitude, my body felt at peace, and I gave thanks to Heaven for sending her to help me.

My last thoughts were for my poor mother who – had she been able to see me – would surely have been completely satisfied with my conduct.

In the morning, when we awoke, my cousins and my aunt were fresher than the rose on the thorn. None of them made any mention of the previous evening's events. As we stood on the terrace, the sun warmed us through our dressing-gowns. I could hear the birds singing away merrily in the trees.

'I must get the picnic ready!' aunt Clara told us. 'Sylvia, get dressed and go for a walk in the grounds. We'll meet up by the front steps at eleven o'clock.'

Véronique and Lucile told me about their friends while my aunt and the servant-girl prepared our open-air meal. I was listening to my cousins at the same time as paying attention to my aunt's voice. And so it was that in a lightning-flash of the mind, a certain Olivier de Gastignes became inextricably linked with the magnificence of sliced beef in jelly. A girl called Anne-Marie Romécourt took on the scent of a raspberry wine which my aunt recommended should be served chilled. All my senses were sharpened by my cheerful mood, and deep in my heart a little tune was playing. Newly enriched by my first evening's lesson, I felt free, absolved from all sin. I couldn't help telling my cousins how much I wanted to run down to the lake.

'May we, Mother?'

'Yes, if you hurry up! The colonel would not forgive us if we were late.'

Véronique and Lucile led me down towards the lawn. I ran with them, and our clothes flapped behind us like wings. Then my cousins stopped at the jetty which they used as a diving-board, and their clothes fell at their feet.

I took off my dressing-gown, then the nightdress which aunt Clara had lent me. Then I did as I was bidden, and dived naked into the water.

At boarding-school, our headmistress, Mme Hartmann, would have taken a dim view of such Biblical attire, and yet I had never bathed in deeper or sweeter waters! I no longer listened to my cousins, or answered their laughter: I was too profoundly moved by my discovery. The water flowed smoothly around my body, caressing the undersides of my breasts which with each stroke were lifted back into the coolest touch of invisible hands. My thighs parted and fast-receding silkiness slid between them, chilling my most secret place, taking my breath away, numbing my mind. I turned over and floated on my back, gazing up into the blue sky, marvelling at the fine, interwoven threads of foliage, and branches above me. Suddenly, I saw in this celestial network the image of all the veins and blood-vessels which criss-crossed within my body. For the first time, I was taking part in the whole of nature, in the waters of the lake, in the sky's clouds, and in the leaves of the trees – and I understood how someone might be a nymph, a goddess, a swan or a reed, for my heart was overflowing with love for creation in all its many forms.

Lucile's voice dragged me back from my dream.

'Be careful, Sylvia, you're drifting off. Don't go onto the island, Gaston is there!'

My cousins had climbed out onto the bank. The golden hue of Lucile's body and the whiteness of Véronique's formed a delightful tableau against the background of greenery.

'We're going back,' shouted Véronique. 'Don't hang around, and don't go onto the island. Gaston is there.'

'But who is Gaston?' I shouted.

Before my cousins could reply, a man's voice, full of respect, murmured behind me:

'I am Gaston, Mademoiselle.'

I turned my head and saw that I had drifted close to the island. Standing in the middle of the bushes was a bearded, red-haired gardener, as startled as a faun. His hat was in his hand, and he greeted me respectfully.

At first, the sight of him made me smile, and then – remembering the advice which my cousins had repeated and noticing the faun's sly expression – I became frightened. As I swam rapidly towards the house, my bottom poked up in the air, and I realised with embarrassment that Gaston must be able to see my backside shooting up out of the water then disappearing from sight like an inconsistent marker-buoy.

Once I was in the bathroom, feeling the shower's delicious needles bruising my flesh, I realised suddenly what I had seen through the bushes and apparently sticking out of Gaston's apron: it was an enormous Garden Boquet, which I had then taken for some fruit growing in the undergrowth.

My aunt had laid out a dress for me on my bed: it was made of Vichy fabric, patterned with black and white squares. Once I was dressed, I looked at myself and saw how out-of-date my outfit looked. I smiled at this bare-armed lady, whose Peter Pan collar and discreetly-buttoned bodice reduced the voluptuousness of what they were covering up. Aunt Clara had supplied the finishing-touch to my outfit by providing a hat. I covered my hair with the plain straw hunting-hat and decided that I was ready to take to the road.

In the gardens, I met uncle Fred. I blushed momentarily, as I recalled all that he had taught me the previous evening, but my embarrassment melted away as he kissed me on the cheek.

'You're as fresh as a daisy, my little girl. I hope that your first day here will be a good one and that you will find ways to amuse yourself here at Charme.'

My uncle was carrying a stack of gardening tools. I asked him what he was doing.

'I'm off to prune the gooseberry bushes. If you'd like to help, come along with me.'

Whilst Fred wielded his secateurs confidently, chopping off the useless suckers, I gathered up the little hard globes, which drummed on the bottom of the bucket as I dropped them in. It seemed as though the secateur was cutting first one thread, then another, inside my heart, and the impact of the gooseberries against the bottom of the pail marked stages in the fall of whatever it was that my uncle was cutting inside me, invisibly: the last traces of my former upbringing, the death-throes of my childhood.

Aunt Clara was calling me from the front steps; if I hadn't been afraid of being seen, I would have obeyed the urge I felt to let my body rise up into the air, like a child's balloon when you break off the string.

My aunt was thrilled to see me so happy. She showed me the brand-new bicycle which had been bought for me. Already my cousins were pedalling away into the distance, crushing the gravel of the drive beneath the wheels of their machines. Just as I was going to get onto my bicycle, my aunt advised me:

'Don't sit on your dress, or you'll crease it. Let it fall around the saddle, like this.'

Underneath her white flannel skirt with its pressed pleats, I saw a little navy-blue underskirt which matched her blouse. This blouse was fitted close to her shapely bosom, just like the tight underskirt which framed my aunt's plump backside as she sat on the saddle.

When it was my turn to cover the saddle with my dress I grabbed hold of my underskirt as well, and without intending to, I found myself sitting on the leather itself, with the point of the saddle in between my thighs. My clumsiness was hardly worth mentioning, but soon I was afraid that my sense of shame would be written all over my face: every time I pushed the pedal down, the intruder's nose tried to force an entry. At first this sensation embarrassed me, then – as my movements fell into a rhythmic pattern – transferred itself to a place where it produced a mood of sweet compliance. It was in this state of mind that I followed the three cyclists onto a little shady path where birds twittered gaily.

Each bump in the road made my rounded breasts quiver and made the saddle-tip which was so unsettling me leap forward. I felt at the same time stimulated by the air rising from the undergrowth, and weakened by the warmth which my enthusiastic movements commanded: I was both giving myself up to the pleasure of this part of the countryside, and also withdrawn within myself. The instrument which was begging for my attention soon made me yield to it: to delay its victory, I stood up on the pedals and managed to tuck my underskirt under me as I sat down. And so the breadth of my vision was reduced and I was able to devote myself entirely to examining what was surrounding me.

'We're going to the home of the Gastignes – Château Robïnshora,' my aunt told me. 'They have two daughters around your age. Their father is Colonel in charge of

Rivers, Lakes and Forests. He will show you some wild boars which he keeps in a cage.'

Why was it that, as soon as I heard the name of this animal, I immediately imagined its hard, hairy skin under my buttocks and its hot snout between my thighs? As though I had been stung by a wasp, I suddenly leapt up. I sat up very straight, pedalled furiously and overtook my cousins, trying to get away from this horrible image – I had seen myself completely naked, rolled around in a field of nettles by a wild boar which was trying repeatedly to force open my thighs with its snout. Like a madwoman, I was rolling down the sloping path.

I heard my aunt cry out:

'Look out, Sylvia!'

But branches, sky, brambles – all were jumbled up in front of me, and I lost control of the handlebars. I glided through the air, head-first and arms in front of my face, down into a ravine.

The fall left me dazed. Alas, the burning sensation which was biting into my arms and my buttocks made me realise that this time I had fallen into a patch of very real nettles! My dress had lifted up at the back of these cruel plants – no doubt spurred on by the bounty offered to them – which had rushed forward to plant their stinging lips upon my backside.

Up above me, on the pathway, my aunt and Lucile were looking for a way to get down and help me. Véronique asked me if I had hurt myself. I saw all of this in a flash when I managed to stand up again. On discovering the slope which led down from the path to me, I thought that I might have been killed, but whilst I was uninjured, I could feel fire whipping at my arse. I looked over my shoulder to assess the damage.

'If you've been stung by the nettles, slap yourself to make the blood circulate – the pain will go away!' Aunt Clara told me.

Treating pain with pain seemed a strange system to me, but I put my trust in my aunt and gave my buttocks a series of noisy slaps which made them burn even more.

However, what she had said would happen, did: the nettle-stings were obliterated as I carefully covered everywhere that my hand could reach with a sheet of burning red. I was distracted from my activities by deep sighing and by a grunting noise. Looking behind me, I saw a jet of milky beads shoot out from the branches, whilst in the midst of the bushes a pink head – just like Papa Boquet's – was being violently shaken about by a gloved hand! I stood there dumbfounded, with my skirt in the air. All I could see amongst the foliage was this spitting cup-and-ball, held by a buttercup-yellow glove. Suddenly another glove parted the leaves and I saw a man's head, topped with a riding hat!

I was horrified, and hurriedly tried to climb the slope, aided in my efforts by pain and shame. Soon I reached the pathway, and fell into aunt Clara's arms.

My cousins found novel ways of comforting me. Lucile ran her tongue gently over the grazes on my arms, aunt Clara took a new pair of stockings out of a saddle-bag (mine had got torn), I was given a sugar-lump soaked in alcohol to crunch, I was made to lie down on the mossy ground, my calves were massaged, and then my aunt lifted up my dress to see if the medicine I had been given had worked. She decided that its effects were not good enough.

'There are some blisters here and there which you couldn't reach. I'll cover them up for you.'

My cousins agreed, and I was given a new beating which made me cry and produced a stirring in the bushes opposite. My cousins took no heed of it; nor did my aunt, who kissed me sweetly and helped me to my feet. I then saw the same white beads shooting out of the undergrowth, the same buttercup-yellow glove moving about and the same black riding-hat disappearing into the branches.

My bottom was so inflamed that it would have been sheer torture to sit on my saddle; so aunt Clara asked her daughters to go on ahead to the château, and I walked along with my bicycle. My aunt did the same, and she did her best to make me forget the accident.

Thanks to her kindness, the fall and the blisters, the mysterious white jets, the slaps and the tears all disappeared from my thoughts. I was once again won over by pleasure. My aunt painted a witty portrait of the ridiculous things which had been suffered by people I did not yet know, but whom I was about to meet at Robïnshora.

'Colonel de Gastignes has a peculiarity,' she told me. 'He's called Lord because he gets all his clothes in London and carries his affectation to the point of having all his new clothes worn first by his valet. Good forms demand that one's appearance should be slightly shabby – a sort of aristocratic weariness. And so you will often see the Colonel in an old riding-habit tailored by Grisby and Murrow, and his riding-hat comes from Lock's.'

'His riding-hat!' I exclaimed.

'What's the matter? Have you never seen one?'

'Oh yes, in fact I just have . . .!'

I was terrified. And so the Colonel, Comte de Gastignes, had twice seen my enormous, naked backside slapped until it was fiery red, and this sight had brought a tear to Papa Boquet's eye!

News of my fall reached Robïnshora before we did. Everyone showed a very friendly interest in me. Olivier de Gastignes, who was a good-looking man, suggested that I should tidy myself up in his sister's room, and Lucile took me there. My aunt and Véronique walked over towards the lawns where other people were waiting.

After the heat of the day outside, I was startled by the cool air wafting down the corridors of the château; my arms were covered in goose-pimples, and I felt as though I were walking along stark naked; our voices echoed around the vaulted ceilings as though we were in a church; along the passage walls, ancestral portraits watched me. Some wore ruffs whilst others had frilled shirts; some were bearded and some were clean shaven – but all of them looked at me with the Colonel's dark eyes!

When we reached the room, Lucile advised me to have a bath, and she ran the water for me.

'Olivier's sister is spending the holidays in England,' she

told me. 'Today you shall see Romuald, his cousin. He's as ugly as sin but he's witty.'

I caught sight of my moss-covered body in the mirror. I looked back over my shoulder: what a sorry sight! My nether cheeks hung heavy and shone a burning, brilliant shade of scarlet. Gingerly, I ran my hand lightly over the burning flesh, but could not soothe it. However, the cool water which Lucile poured over my shoulders made me feel much better. The tips of my breasts had gone hard. Lucile laughed.

'We shall have to warm them up a bit,' she said, planting a kiss on each of them in turn.

I was just threatening to punish her for such impudence when we were alerted by a noise coming from a neighbouring study. We opened the door and looked into the room, where we saw an upturned chair. A curtain hung across the far end of the room: we lifted it and found ourselves in the chill air of a corridor.

'Was it a ghost? The castle is full of them.'

'If it is a ghost,' I replied, 'he must live on a diet of milk.'

My cousin looked down and saw the pale drops of liquid which stood out against the parquet floor. Blushing for no apparent reason, she dragged me away, saying:

'Get dressed quickly.'

The château Robïnshora was built from light-red brick and stood in the midst of lawns and in front of tall, leafy trees which looked like moving mountains as they swayed in the wind. This was exactly the intention of Louis XIII, from whom the Gastignes had got their taste for hunting. This distant ancestry explained their arrogance, which was recalled by the mocking motto inscribed on the family coat of arms: 'Trousse qui veut. Boute qui peut!' (He who drops his breeks must watch his cheeks!)

On the lawn, a dozen or so people were chatting. Olivier de Gastignes introduced me to Romuald Bedford, his English cousin. He was covered in reddish spots, and had uncontrollable hair and a mouth full of irregular teeth, but you couldn't help liking him because of his slender figure and open expression. Arnaud de Saint-Alban and Henri de

Montèche were both students at the Ecole Polytechnique, and had been determined to dress up in their uniforms for the occasion. One couldn't help but notice their tight-buttoned necks and small heads, as though their heads and necks were emerging from their uniform collars under the immense pressure generated by straining hooks and eyes and belt-buckles tightened to the last notch. Saint-Alban was wearing gold-rimmed spectacles which gave him a disturbingly fixed expression. Montèche had a tortoiseshell-rimmed monocle wedged under one eyebrow: this set one half of his face into immovable stiffness. These two young fellows greeted me politely: with their cocked hats tucked underneath their arms, they looked like figures out of an engraving. Their reserved manner told me that they were 'of good breeding', as my poor mother used to say, and I was delighted by this discovery.

François de Turaine was the last young gallant. Like Olivier he was twenty and was taking a forestry course at the same college. He was paying court to my cousin Lucile, who – for her part – looked upon him favourably.

It was then that we saw Yvonne de Gastignes, the Colonel's younger daughter, coming towards us with her friend Anne-Marie Romécourt, whom Véronique had told me about. Both of them were charming, pretty and slender and were obviously quite at ease. I felt terribly lumpish next to them: I saw my cousins conversing with both of them effortlessly, and as for me – I hadn't a clue what to say. The best thing for me to do, I thought to myself, is to sit down on the grass, nibble a flower and let my mind drift away so that I look the picture of naturalness and enticing charm. I set about doing this, but I had hardly sat down when I jumped up with a cry of pain: the weight of my backside had crushed a thistle, and its spikes had immediately and gleefully embedded themselves in my flesh.

Concerned by the instinctive movement of my hand towards the site of the pain, people gathered round me, turned me towards the sun and made me bend forward. Arnaud de Saint-Alban adjusted his spectacles to see if any of the spikes were still attached to my dress and, finding one, he grabbed hold of it. I felt him pinch me and this made me kick out wildly. My boot hit Saint-Alban squarely, knocking him over, and his hat rolled away. Véronique, who was holding me as I bent over, was unable to steady me and so I pitched forward, head-first, onto the ground and then rolled over onto my back. In the speed of my fall I lost control, and was horrified to feel my legs lifting up: I realised that I was baring my fanny and the round, scarlet mass of my buttocks to the flabbergasted throng!

Olivier de Gastignes was the first to comfort me. I apologised to Arnaud de Saint-Alban, who considerately blamed his own clumsiness: this gave me a chance to notice his speech impediment.

'Without my glatheth,' he told me, 'I'm ath blind ath a bat. Tho when I took hold of the end of the thithle, I was thurprithed to feel a little bit of your thelf between my fingerth ath well ...'

He waddled about like an adorable simpleton, and I thought to myself that his outfit must feel heavy because it was so tight – a fact which was proved by the way the material of his trousers bulged out, obviously because of some knife he'd slipped into his pocket in anticipation of our open-air meal.

We set out quickly. Servants had already delivered the foodstuffs to a spot chosen by the Colonel, by the side of a lake. Olivier de Gastignes walked by my side and talked to me about Switzerland, where he knew I had been at school.

'From now on, that country will take on a whole new importance for me. When I met you just now, I could see that you had been properly fed. I'm only attracted to plump girls and I hate this fashion which turns girls into boys. When they're flat-chested and straight-up-and-down like that, no one could possibly desire them.'

This direct compliment surprised me, but I thought it proper to respond in the way I had been taught by our teacher of etiquette, Miss Brenda.

'I am pleased that I suit your tastes: for you are the embodiment of all mine. You have the youth, good breeding and wealth which I had hoped to find grouped together in one man.'

'Since we are both satisfied with each other,' he continued with a smile, 'do not refuse me the pleasures which I myself am ready to bestow on you.'

'What pleasures are you talking about?'

'I want to have another look at what I glimpsed a little while ago, only this time I want to take my time.'

I was offended by such impudence, so I did not reply and went back to join my aunt.

As I walked away, did I really hear Olivier murmuring to himself:

'Whether you want to or not, my beauty, you shall soon bare your arse to me . . .'

This remark – which I could not have imagined – gave me a new insight into the Gastignes. This family of hunters was in reality made up of wolves.

The Colonel made a great impression on me. He was tall and thin, with an aquiline nose and a faraway voice, and he ended each phrase by drawling 'what': which turned his conversation into a series of questions. In my eyes, he was the very epitome of distinction. A signet ring on his finger accentuated the nobility of his long hands which punctuated everything he said with an agreeable pantomime.

When he caught sight of me, he took off his riding-hat to reveal a gleaming pate. There was a mocking gleam in his dark eyes as his deep voice murmured:

'If I didn't know that I had never made your acquaintance, I should say, Mademoiselle, that I had already met you, for your face reminds me of another, what?'

Was this a way to tell me that my face resembled the object of all my torments? This resemblance must have become even more marked, because I felt myself blushing with shame. But Véronique and Yvonne de Gastignes were already leading me away. I was made to sit down on a Scottish wool blanket in a bold check pattern, next to Olivier and François de Turaine.

The eatables emerged from the baskets, and three man-servants in blue aprons worked miracles around us. They set out trays to which the flower-patterned plates added a cheerful note. In front of us, the waters of the pond rippled gently, the leaves on the trees protected us from the sun, and a breeze freshened our bare arms. My cousins had sat down cross-legged without revealing any part of their backsides. I had preferred to kneel down, and then sit back on my heels to prevent any accident. François de Turaine, who was a tall, bronzed lad with wild eyes, buttered a piece of French toast for me and asked me about my taste in films. His dream was to become a film-maker, and he thought I was well suited to portray one of his heroines. I confessed that my experience of the film world was limited to evenings at Mme Hartmann's: a few Charlie Chaplin romps and a film of the headmistress's cousin climbing the Jungfrau – which we had seen at least a hundred times and which I could have recited from memory.

Shortly afterwards, I saw Anne-Marie Romécourt lean over towards the chicken fricassee and as she did so, she revealed two white, hard breasts which wobbled about freely in the depths of her bodice. Had she too dispensed with covering her most secret places, like my cousins and myself? Perhaps it was a custom among country girls and not a simple whim reserved by my uncle for his wife and daughters?

I turned towards aunt Clara. She was leaning back against a tree and chatting with the Colonel. I saw her raise one of her legs so that she could rest the plate she was holding, on her knee. This movement uncovered all the fullness of her naked thigh above her stocking, and a little patch of shadow within, under the flounces of her dress. Henri de Montèche and Arnaud de Saint-Alban immediately lay down flat on their stomachs, like lizards, and ate their food at ground level, looking upwards at my aunt's thigh – yet no one showed the slightest surprise at their posture or the direction of their gaze.

Olivier de Gastignes poured me out a glass of white wine mixed with ice water, which made me more giddy. Lucile had monopolised François de Turaine's attentions, whilst Véronique and her friend Romécourt were laughing with

165

the little Bedford fellow. How relaxed well-bred people are when their pleasures are so discreet! I said to myself. On this picnic, the setting chosen by the Colonel adds the charms of a constantly changing landscape to the pleasures of food.

I turned towards my aunt to share my happiness with her. As she spoke, she moved her knee from right to left to give herself some air – something which the bright-red faces of the Polytechnic students at her feet seemed to be deprived of. Olivier de Gastignes was telling me how, in the autumn, he had hunted teal and moorhens on the lake. Suddenly, I was alerted by a tickling sensation. I was still sitting on my heels, with my skirt pulled tightly around me, and I did not understand how a blade of grass could have slipped through my dress and was tickling my hip. As I ate a dish of ice-cream, I listened to Olivier's hunting tales, but I could not suppress the sudden little starts caused by the little intruder, which was now at the top of my thigh and was moving about over my skin.

With my knees pressed tightly together and my jaws clamped on a mouthful of sorbet which was chilling my teeth, my mind followed the flight of the wild ducks and the onward progression of the grass-stalk as it tickled me. Suddenly the evidence came to light: in the folds of the blanket I caught sight of a dozen or so ants, running about in all directions!

Luckily, the panic didn't start with me but with a shout from my cousin Lucile, who leapt to her feet:

'We're on an ants' nest!'

All the ladies were now on their feet, jumping up and down and giving little cries. The teal-hunter, and film-maker, the Englishman, the two lizards, the Colonel and even the waiters rushed to our aid and in doing so, actually made things more difficult for us; one grabbed our arms, another pushed us forwards. This caused Véronique to lose her balance, and she staggered and fell into the blackcurrant ice-cream. Her dress lifted up right to the very top of her thighs. Saint-Albaun rushed over to her, saying:

'I can thee a great big pink ant!'

Pulling up her dress completely, he uncovered my cousin's backside and – on account of his extreme short-sight – pressed his spectacles right up against it. Anne-Marie, who was scratching herself all over, opened her bodice; with the sudden release of pressure, we saw two beautiful fat, pink-tipped bubbies dancing about: and Henri de Montèche fixed his attentive, monocled gaze on them. Yvonne de Gastignes was just as covered in ants as we were, and lifted her dress to reveal a pair of lace panties which Monsieur de Turaine hurriedly pulled down to her ankles. My aunt had bared her legs, and was allowing the Colonel to examine her: he was looking all over her belly for a venturesome ant. I hardly had time to see these little tableaux; as soon as Lucile cried out, Olivier had come to my rescue. He seized my wrist and pulled at me so violently that I found myself on my knees, with my dress pulled up onto my shoulders, and I was unable to hide the mass of naked flesh which his hand was caressing.

And so, in an instant, all six of us found ourselves with our dresses hitched up, the wind blowing up our cunts, on view and at the mercy of whoever chose to touch us! I watched my aunt so that I could base my own behaviour on hers, and I was surprised to see all these gentlemen standing around us, with their Papa Boquet in their hands! Even the waiters had lifted up their big aprons so they wouldn't be in the way. The jets which shot out of them no doubt sent the ants packing, for that was the end of the incident. I don't know how long this downpour lasted, but our defenders were so diligent that we quickly found ourselves on our feet again, dazed but unhurt. The Colonel comforted us with a compliment.

'Ladies, when one sees the soft, sweet areas where those little explorers wanted to venture, one can hardly blame them. Let's leave them to it, and have our coffee back at the château!'

Laughing to hide our embarrassment, and surrounded by our gallant protectors' concern, we recovered our composure.

'Don't you think what happened was rather unseemly?' I couldn't stop myself asking as I passed Clara.

'Only evil minds are unseemly. Look at nature and behave accordingly.'

'It provides us with our best role-model,' added the Colonel.

I felt comforted by this.

Coffee was served in the library. Outside, the heat had mounted and reached boiling-point. To occupy the few hours until the temperature cooled down, we had a choice of card-games to play – Pope Joan or piquet. A few people, like aunt Clara and the Colonel, withdrew. Others chose music or reading. And the time until we went home passed without further incident.

When we got back to Charme, I had to tell uncle Fred all about our day. He was entertained by my mishaps. Then, when we were all in the drawing-room, he announced:

'In Sylvia's honour, I shall make an exception to our rule. Although it is Monday, tonight we shall stage a little drill which is necessary for her upbringing.

'The golden rule of all morality is never to force other people. As long as you keep to this condition, you have a claim to affirm your rights. If your tastes offend your neighbour, never impose them. If those that they show you displease you, then you must not go along with them. All the conflicts of our species arise from the fact that one person forces another. Now, the richness of individuals is such that everyone can find his or her match. And when that happens, equal exchange replaces compulsion, and harmony replaces subjection. The teachings which I give you are to prepare you for a perfect understanding with whoever Heaven intends for you. Now, in turn, I want to carry out the autumn leaves drill.'

Véronique carefully parted the cheeks of her mother's Montespan and looked at the amber-coloured orifice which evoked the russet shades of autumn. In my mind's eye, I saw the great forests which surrounded the boarding-school at the moment when sunshine followed the October rains: when the landscape gleamed in shades of copper and gold. Véronique's tongue brought a little moisture to this autumnal spot, producing murmurs of approval from my aunt. Lucile did the same for her sister and I stationed myself in the necessary position to do the same. Lucile took as much pleasure in my caresses as I afterwards experienced when I received hers.

'Since you are now wide awake, send your Josephines to sleep before you go to bed,' advised my uncle.

My aunt and my cousins placed a finger on their secret flowers and rubbed them gently. Uncle Fred watched us. He advised me to pinch the tips of my breasts at the same time, and immediately I felt a greater sense of well-being. In this way, we all calmed ourselves and wished each other good night.

The next day, Olivier de Gastignes came to Charme and asked for my hand in marriage! My uncle gave his consent and a month later, I found myself legally and completely at the disposal of this determined young man. In spite of my cousins' congratulations, I was dreading going to live at Robïnshora, in the Colonel's château.

On the morning of my marriage, my aunt – aided by the dressmaker who had come from Paris – put the finishing touches to my embroidered lace gown.

'What a pretty bride!' exclaimed uncle Fred as he came into my room.

He sent the dressmaker out and looked at me with affection.

'When a child leaves us, it is customary to say farewell. In our own way. Sylvia, bend over the bed.'

My aunt lifted up my dress with its train, and revealed white stockings, crowned by my beautiful Montespan, on which my uncle rained down five hundred hard slaps as proof of his affection. My longest-ever beating! When the old Delage took me off to the church at Charme, I had some difficulty in keeping my bottom on the seat.

The wedding breakfast took place at Robïnshora. All our gallants from the picnic were there, but – before we sat down to eat – my new husband showed me his rooms.

Without further ado, I made the acquaintance of his riding-whip, which he used to whip my thighs and buttocks ten times! I was choking on my tears after this special 'Welcome Home', but at his request I had to kiss my tyrant's hand. I then noticed the red face of my father-in-law, who was watching us through a half-opened door. The bride who took the place of honour at the table was well-spanked, well-whipped, had bare thighs and reddened eyes.

Without seeming to be moved by these avatars, I fulfilled all my obligations perfectly during the course of the day, smiling twenty times for the *Vogue* photographer who had come from Paris to take pictures which would later be printed in the magazine.

Luckily, as the months went by the manifestations of authority became fewer. One evening, the Colonel left our world to go elsewhere and see if the angels were anything like the beautiful creatures he had loved on Earth. And for the last twenty years I have been Comtesse Sylvia de Gastignes.

Thanks to my education in Charme, I think I have been just as agreeable a mistress to my husband as he has been a perfect lover to me. We both laughed at my naiveté when I discovered the causes and effects of events which had hitherto been incomprehensible to me. With Olivier, I share everything: pleasures, curiosity, research, work, travel. As my husband got older, he turned towards philosophy. He went off to India to look for a new way of life and brought back Tantric teachings which he passed on to me. I learned how to speak in tongues, how consciously to hold back my orgasm, and how to develop my powers of concentration. With love, we mingled our breath in complicated postures to celebrate the rite of Maithuna, which reproduces the sacred union of Shiva and Shakti. Our efforts enabled us to reach ecstasies of a higher order; and the perfect union of our bodies and our souls set us on the path that leads to God.

When the time came for me to give my husband his freedom so that marriage should weigh less heavily upon him, I did it without difficulty. I know that he attracts ever-younger and ever-prettier disciples, but when he returns from his escapades it is here at Robïnshora, and with me, that he finds happiness.

Our only regret is that we never had children. That is why I have written down my memoirs here, so that young minds can retain their example and may – by putting them into practice – attain the benefits which accompany them.

NEW BOOKS

Coming up from Nexus and Black Lace

There are three Nexus titles published in March

The Black Widow *by Lisette Ashton*
March 1999   Price £5.99   ISBN: 0 352 33338 3

Spurned by her husband, and cheated of her heritage, the Black Widow feels justified in seeking revenge. Determined to lay claim to Elysian Fields, a health farm with a unique doctrine of sensual pleasure and erotic stimulation, the Black Widow wants what is rightfully hers. Indulging a new-found passion for sexual domination, she is only too pleased to deal with those that get in her way. Punishments are cruel and explicit as she forces subordinates to do her bidding. Caught in the middle of the hostile takeover, Jo Valentine finds herself entangled in the Black Widow's web. By the author of *The Black Room* and *Amazon Slave*.

The Reluctant Virgin *by Kendal Grahame*
March 1999   Price £5.99   ISBN: 0 352 33339 1

The beautiful Karina Devonside is due to inherit a fortune on her twenty-first birthday, but she is far from happy. Unlike her naughty best friend Sandy, she is still a virgin, and circumstances are conspiring to keep her that way. But Sandy's tales of sluttish behaviour have been driving Karina wild for too long now – who will she choose to help her sate her lust? By the author of *The Training of Fallen Angels* and *The Warrior Queen*.

Choosing Lovers for Justine *by Aran Ashe*
March 1999   Price £5.99   ISBN: 0 352 33351 0

Chosen to live a life according to discipline and subservience, the young Justine is introduced to a succession of lovers. Each one has favoured methods of taking pleasure from her willing body – pleasure which is often found through the demands of pain and submission. Presided over by her strict guardian Julia, we follow Justine's initiation into a world of obedience, dominated by the less than genteel ladies and gentlemen of the Edwardian well-to-do. This novel, by the author of *The Handmaidens* and *Citadel of Servitude*, is the second in a series of Nexus Classics – dedicated to putting the finest works of erotic fiction back in print.

There are three Nexus titles published in April

Displays of Innocents by Lucy Golden

April 1999   Price £5.99   ISBN: 0 352 33342 1

The twelve stories in this collection reveal the experiences of those who dare to step outside the familiar bounds of everyday life. Irene is called for an interview, but has never been examined as thoroughly as this; Gemma cannot believe the demands made by her new clients, a respectable middle-aged couple; Helen learns that the boss's wife has an intimate way of demonstrating her authority. For some, it widens their horizons; for others it is an agony never to be repeated. For all twelve, it is a tale of intense erotic power.

Disciples of Shame by Stephanie Calvin

April 1999   Price £5.99   ISBN: 0 352 33343 X

Inspired by her grandfather's memoirs, the young and beautiful Amelia decides to begin her own erotic adventures. She soon draws all around her into her schemes as they help her to act out her most lewd fantasies – among others her best friend, Alice, who loves to be told what to do, and her shy aunt, Susan, who needs to be persuaded. All her friends take part in her increasingly bizarre games, before the final, most perverse drama unfolds.

The Institute by Maria del Rey

April 1999   Price £5.99   ISBN: 0 352 33352 9

Set in a strange institute for the treatment of delinquent girls between the ages of eighteen and twenty-one, this is the story of Lucy, a naughty young woman who is sentenced to be rehabilitated. Their disciplinary methods are not what she has been led to expect, however – they are, in fact, decidedly strange. This is the third in a series of Nexus Classics – dedicated to bringing the finest works of erotic fiction to a new audience.

BLACK
lace

The Top of Her Game by Emma Holly
March 1999   Price £5.99   ISBN: 0 352 33337 5
Successful dominatrix Julia Mueller has been searching all her life for
a man who is too tough to be tamed. But when she locks horns with
a no-nonsense Montana rancher, will she discover the perfect balance
between domination and surrender, or will her dark side win out?

Raw Silk by Lisabet Sarai
March 1999   Price £5.99   ISBN: 0 352 33336 7
When software engineer Kate O'Neil leaves her lover David to take
a job in Bangkok, she becomes sexually involved with two very different men: a kinky member of the Thai aristocracy and the charis-
matic proprietor of a sex bar. When David arrives in Thailand, Kate
realises she must choose between three very different men. She invites
all three to join her in a sexual adventure that finally makes clear to
her what she really wants and needs.

Stand and Deliver by Helena Ravenscroft
April 1999   Price £5.99   ISBN: 0 352 33340 5
It's the 18th century. Lydia Fitzgerald finds herself helplessly drawn
to Drummond, a handsome highwayman. This occurs despite the fact
that she is the ward of his brother, Valerian, who controls the
Hawkesworth estate. There, Valerian and his beautiful mistress initi-
ate Lydia's seduction and, though she is in love with Drummond,
Lydia is unable to resist the experimentation they offer.

Haunted by Laura Thornton
April 1999   Price £5.99   ISBN: 0 352 33341 3
A modern-day Gothic story set in both England and New York.
Sasha Hayward is an American woman whose erotic obsession with
a long-dead pair of lovers leads her on a steamy and evocative search.
Seeking out descendants of the enigmatic pair, Sasha consummates
her obsession in a series of stangely perverse encounters related to
this haunting mystery.

NEXUS BACKLIST

All books are priced £5.99 unless another price is given. If a date is supplied, the book in question will not be available until that month in 1999.

CONTEMPORARY EROTICA

AMAZON SLAVE	Lisette Ashton		
BAD PENNY	Penny Birch		Feb
THE BLACK GARTER	Lisette Ashton		
THE BLACK WIDOW	Lisette Ashton		Mar
BOUND TO OBEY	Amanda Ware		
BRAT	Penny Birch		May
CHAINS OF SHAME	Brigitte Markham		
DARK DELIGHTS	Maria del Rey		
DARLINE DOMINANT	Tania d'Alanis		
A DEGREE OF DISCIPLINE	Zoe Templeton	£4.99	
DISCIPLES OF SHAME	Stephanie Calvin		Apr
THE DISCIPLINE OF NURSE RIDING	Yolanda Celbridge		
DISPLAYS OF INNOCENTS	Lucy Golden		Apr
EDUCATING ELLA	Stephen Ferris	£4.99	
EMMA'S SECRET DOMINATION	Hilary James	£4.99	
EXPOSING LOUISA	Jean Aveline		Jan
FAIRGROUND ATTRACTIONS	Lisette Ashton		
JULIE AT THE REFORMATORY	Angela Elgar	£4.99	
LINGERING LESSONS	Sarah Veitch		Jan
A MASTER OF DISCIPLINE	Zoe Templeton		
THE MISTRESS OF STERNWOOD GRANGE	Arabella Knight		

ONE WEEK IN THE PRIVATE HOUSE	Esme Ombreux	£4.99	
PENNY IN HARNESS	Penny Birch		
THE RELUCTANT VIRGIN	Kendal Grahame		Mar
THE REWARD OF FAITH	Elizabeth Bruce	£4.99	
RITES OF OBEDIENCE	Lindsay Gordon		
RUE MARQUIS DE SADE	Morgana Baron		
'S' – A STORY OF SUBMISSION	Philippa Masters	£4.99	
'S' – A JOURNEY INTO SERVITUDE	Philippa Masters		
THE SCHOOLING OF STELLA	Yolanda Celbridge	£4.99	
THE SUBMISSION OF STELLA	Yolanda Celbridge		Feb
SECRETS OF THE WHIPCORD	Michaela Wallace	£4.99	
THE SUBMISSION GALLERY	Lindsay Gordon		Jun
SUSIE IN SERVITUDE	Arabella Knight		
TAKING PAINS TO PLEASE	Arabella Knight		Jun
A TASTE OF AMBER	Penny Birch		
THE TEST	Nadine Somers		Jan
THE TRAINING OF FALLEN ANGELS	Kendal Grahame	£4.99	
VIRGINIA'S QUEST	Katrina Young	£4.99	

ANCIENT & FANTASY SETTINGS

THE CASTLE OF MALDONA	Yolanda Celbridge	£4.99	
NYMPHS OF DIONYSUS	Susan Tinoff	£4.99	
THE WARRIOR QUEEN	Kendal Grahame		

EDWARDIAN, VICTORIAN & OLDER EROTICA

ANNIE AND THE COUNTESS	Evelyn Culber		
THE CORRECTION OF AN ESSEX MAID	Yolanda Celbridge		
MISS RATTAN'S LESSON	Yolanda Celbridge		
PRIVATE MEMOIRS OF A KENTISH HEADMISTRESS	Yolanda Celbridge	£4.99	
THE TRAINING OF AN ENGLISH GENTLEMAN	Yolanda Celbridge		May
SISTERS OF SEVERCY	Jean Aveline	£4.99	

SAMPLERS & COLLECTIONS

EROTICON 4	Various		
THE FIESTA LETTERS	ed. Chris Lloyd	£4.99	
NEW EROTICA 4			

NEXUS CLASSICS
A new imprint dedicated to putting the finest works of erotic fiction back in print

THE IMAGE	Jean de Berg	Feb
CHOOSING LOVERS FOR JUSTINE	Aran Ashe	Mar
THE INSTITUTE	Maria del Rey	Apr
AGONY AUNT	G. C. Scott	May
THE HANDMAIDENS	Aran Ashe	Jun

Please send me the books I have ticked above.

Name   ....

Address   ....

                 ....

                 ....

                 .... Post code........................

Send to: **Cash Sales, Nexus Books, Thames Wharf Studios, Rainville Road, London W6 9HT**

Please enclose a cheque or postal order, made payable to **Nexus Books**, to the value of the books you have ordered plus postage and packing costs as follows:

UK and BFPO – £1.00 for the first book, 50p for the second book and 30p for each subsequent book to a maximum of £3.00;

Overseas (including Republic of Ireland) – £2.00 for the first book, £1.00 for the second book and 50p for each subsequent book.

If you would prefer to pay by VISA or ACCESS/MASTER-CARD, please write your card number and expiry date here:

....

Please allow up to 28 days for delivery.

Signature ....